Terra Nullius

Also by Margaret Visciglio and published by Ginninderra Press
The Blue Roses of Orroroo
On the Edge

Margaret Visciglio

Terra Nullius

& other stories

To Frank with love

Terra Nullius & other stories
ISBN 978 1 74027 932 1
Copyright © Margaret Visciglio 2015

First published 2015 by
GINNINDERRA PRESS
PO Box 3461 Port Adelaide SA 5015
www.ginninderrapress.com.au

Contents

5

'Not all those who wander are lost'
– J.R.R. Tolkien

Terra Nullius

'Are you here because of the money, Mr Foulkes?' asked young Cowley.

I watched the water reflecting on the cliff face, the light flitting and changing as the trees moved in the warm breeze. I lifted one leg and let the cool water run down it. Almost unbelievable, I thought, that there could be this much water after the desert we had just come through. 'Of course, lad,' I said. 'Isn't that why you're here?'

'I want to get married and buy a little farm near Adelaide,' he said. 'Only I've promised some of the money to my parents, too. They're finding life a bit tough at the moment.'

We were all finding life a bit tough in South Australia this year – 1844. Jobs were in short supply and I was beginning to think it had been a mistake to emigrate. Perhaps Ann was right, we should have stayed back home in Wales, although my daughters Sarah, Ellen and Emma Fortitude were happy here.

The weather in South Australia was certainly better than in Britain. Well, not the weather in the country we had come through to get here. That was what hell must be like, I thought, remembering the vast empty plains where stones alternated with sand and it was almost impossible to find feed for the bullocks. Yes, that was hell. I ducked my head under the water again. And this was heaven.

'They say you were a soldier, Mr Foulkes,' the boy continued.

Why did he have to talk so much? I thought. He's probably lonely. Hasn't learned to be self-sufficient yet. A man learns to be alone in the army. You have to, because there's no knowing when your best mate is going to be killed. Could happen out here, too, come to think of it. A man could die of thirst. Or be speared by the natives if they realise what we're doing to them. And what would happen to Ann and the children then?

'Yes,' I said. 'I was a soldier. India, Canada and then, of course, that war against Napoleon. Spain and Portugal. Badajoz, that was the worst of it.' I shuddered, remembering the fire and the screaming.

'Is that where you got those scars?' he asked.

I lifted an arm, turned it so that I could see the marks. One bullet hole there, one on the leg I had lifted a minute ago, and another where I had caught it in the side. That was the shot that nearly killed me. Only the work of the surgeons and good Spanish wine to disinfect the wound got me through that lot. I had earned the Chelsea pension for those wounds.

Ann thought I would slow down a bit after I was wounded and awarded the pension. I did, for a while, but she's right when she says my worst fault is my wanderlust. I gave her my word that if we migrated to South Australia I would be content to live a quiet life. But I'm not good at keeping my promises. A man gets bored.

She's a great reader, my Ann, She told me about some bloke she had read about in a book – Ulysses, that was his name – who travelled all around the Greek islands and came home to his wife, but then he took off again carrying an oar and telling her that he was going to go inland as far as he could get until he found a place where no one knew what an oar was. Ann says that's what I'm like.

I'm not carrying an oar, but there's a whale boat loaded on the bullock wagon that I'm in charge of. Captain Sturt claims there's an inland sea out here somewhere. Personally, I think he's mad, just like that Ulysses fellow. This water at Depot Glen is about as much water as we're going to find out here in this empty land.

But Captain Sturt's an educated man. I'm just a humble bullock driver and I never rose above the rank of private in the army. Never wanted to. Let others do the commanding, is my motto. It's safer. Well, it's safer if the officers know what they're doing and, to tell the truth, they can make mistakes, too.

'I thought we were going to die out there,' said Cowley. 'It was horrible. No trees, and just endless plains. How do you reckon those natives we saw manage?'

'They'll be managing worse than they were before we came through, poor buggers,' I said. 'We drove horses, bullocks and a mob of sheep through their country, dirtied up their waterholes, shot the kangaroos and emus they were depending on for food. We've done the wrong thing, young Joe, you mark my words. And if this country is opened up, the way the captain is hoping it will be, it'll be the natives that suffer for it.'

'They might be better off if there are people out here,' protested Cowley. 'The natives down in Adelaide get flour and tea given to them.'

'And diseases. And where do they live in Adelaide?' I asked. 'How healthy do they look?'

'In huts out on the edge of town,' admitted the lad. 'Yair, I s'pose they don't look too well off. But that's not our fault, is it? They could move out further if they wanted to. Nobody's really going to come and live out here, though. This country's unbearable.'

'Remember those hills we came over, the place the captain called the Barrier Range?' I asked. 'Those coloured stones the captain and his officers were picking up, did you see them? Minerals, that's what that was. I saw silver there. I've seen silver on the ground in Spain. And those green rocks, those were copper. There could even be gold. Once that news gets back to Adelaide, there'll be prospectors come after us.'

'Where will they get the water?' he asked.

'Take it away from the blacks, same as we did. Water for drinking, water for horses and bullocks and sheep, water to wash in and swim in if there's enough. But there won't be enough for them and for us. Not unless the captain finds that inland sea.'

'You don't believe in the inland sea, Mr Foulkes?'

'No, lad, I don't. If there was an inland sea, would those poor natives be sitting out there, roasting in the sun half-starved? They'd be camped on the edge of it, wouldn't they? Eating oysters and fish and enjoying life.'

'Why aren't they here, then?'

'Because we're here, that's why. They're scared of us. They think we're ghosts with white skins come back from the dead, so they keep out of our way as much as they can. But they've been here. You go up the creek a bit and you'll see carvings on the cliff face. Lewis and a couple of the other blokes carved their initials on that cliff, but you can see the difference.'

'What difference?'

'Lewis's initials are sharp cut. Those old carvings are soft-edged, shiny from time passing. They've been there a long time. After we've gone, the natives will come back here. Trouble is, by then the water will be dirty and they won't be able to use it. No respect, that's what's wrong with us whites. I learned respect in India. When you've got water, you take care of it. You don't put soap into it and ruin it for the ones who come after you. Not when there's not much of it to share.'

We heard shouting. Something was happening.

'It's the captain!' said Joe Cowley. 'He's back. He's probably come to get the boat so we can sail it on the inland sea.'

We threw our clothes on and ran to meet the returning party. Captain Sturt could hardly stand. It was the scurvy, I knew. It's a rotten disease, but it's preventable I had learned in India that you needed to eat leaves or berries (either you watch to see what the natives are eating and you do the same, or you try them out on an animal first, and if the animal doesn't get sick or die, then it's safe to eat them yourself). But the officers would never listen when we men tried to tell them that. That was why the men on our expedition didn't get sick the way the officers did.

And the captain was a very sick man. A brave one, but not a well one. He hadn't found any inland sea which didn't surprise me, although young Joe Cowley was disappointed.

In the end, we launched the whale boat and left it floating in the water at Depot Glen. No captain and no crew. I suppose it sank eventually.

And I went home to Ann and promised that from now on I would lead a quiet life, content to sit by the fire. But a man gets bored…

The Memory Lingers Still

Kneeling in the forlorn patch of lobelias and English daisies that wilted in the hot sun, Charles wondered again what insane decision had brought him to this godforsaken place, so far from the cool, damp country he loved.

His house stood distanced from the others in the new housing development. But there were few houses so far. What trees might once have stood here had been bulldozed. The estate was an open, raw wound, a desolate place of yellowing grass recently grazed by sheep, where one glimpsed the occasional furtive rabbit or fox.

He saw a figure moving towards him through the dry paddocks where the Scotch thistles thrived. Charles could never understand how those things did so well when everything he planted died.

The person, whoever it was, approached Charles's block. The man carried a tin of fluid and a stick and made slow progress, as he continually bent, poked at something on the ground and poured fluid from the tin, emitting cries of 'Got you, you bugger!'

'How yer going?' called the man. 'I'm Bill – live up the road a bit. Reckon you're Charlie, Milly's hubby, aren't yer? Milly came to the wife's Tupperware party.'

'Yes,' said Charles, extending his hand. 'Pleased to meet you. I wonder – what are you doing?'

'It's them bloody trapdoor spiders,' explained Bill. 'Real poisonous, they are. Don't s'pose you know about them – you're a Pommie, aren't yer? Don't s'pose they've got them over there. If the kiddies get bit by them, they're a goner. Whereabouts in England do yer come from, Charlie?'

'Salisbury, United Kingdom, actually,' said Charles.

'Yair?' said Bill. 'Not much imagination, coming from Salisbury UK to Salisbury SA. Well, yez can give me a hand with the trapdoors, Charlie, then I reckon a beer might go down well. What do yez reckon?'

The beer was cold and welcome after the hot work of tramping the vacant blocks, locating the holes in which the trapdoor spiders dwelt, then lifting their little lids with the stick and pouring the contents of Bill's tin (which turned out to be kerosene) into the unfortunate insects' homes.

Somehow the subject of alcoholic beverages other than beer came up, and Bill mentioned that the Polish bloke around the corner had a still, and was brewing up a horrible distillation of potato peels to make vodka.

'The Italian chap I work with makes wine,' ventured Charles. 'He said that he has gallons of it that's gone off and he'll have to get rid of it unless he can find someone with a still. Apparently one can make something called grappa from spoiled wine.'

Bill was ecstatic. 'Listen, mate, you talk to the Itie and I'll have a word with Fred,' he said. 'We'll get this thing organised and we'll all have a share in it. Four ways, I reckon. We'll all be partners.'

Over the following weeks, Bill's shed became a focus of activity. Flagons of vinegary wine lined the shelves labelled 'kero' lest the law somehow discovered the operation. The still stood in a corner with a tarp draped over it.

After his evening meal, Charles would walk up the hill to Bill's shed, where they would be joined by Fred the Pole, who was an expert in the art of distillation and whose complexion already wore a faintly jaundiced tinge to prove it.

The men would sit on up-ended buckets around the still, which was placed on a kero-powered portable stove and from which a hissing sound came, punctuated with occasional pops. They would carefully pour the acrid smelling wine into a funnel at the top of the still and wait until the magical process took place which converted it into pure spirit.

'The first bit is dangerous,' warned Charles, 'and shouldn't be swallowed.' He had read this in a book he had found in the library.

But Fred shrugged. 'For you, perhaps,' he said scornfully, and swallowed the stuff with relish.

From time to time, one or another of them would put a teaspoon under the spout and taste the fluid to check that it was alcohol and not water that flowed. This could, for some esoteric reason known only to the Pole, happen occasionally.

Steam wreathed the shed, evoking in Charles a memory of the mists of his birthplace; and indeed, the mutterings of his partners in crime could have been the invocations of the Druid priests of Stonehenge.

'Could run a jet engine on this,' boasted Bill. 'I put a match to it the other day and it burns with a blue flame. What proof do yez reckon it is, Fred?'

Fred pondered, jaundiced eyes on the still. 'It is one hundred per cent proof,' he answered eventually. 'I, of course, can drink this, but you, you must add some water or something to it.'

'It ought to have a name,' Bill announced. 'Anything as good as this deserves to have a name. You name it, Charlie. You're the one with the education.'

Charles's brain felt as foggy as the atmosphere in the shed. He considered the problem for a few moments. He felt that a noble name was called for, something worthy of the arts of the ancients, something more lofty than grappa or vodka.

He gazed out the shed door from his bucket seat and saw the Southern Cross glistening in the dark southern sky. So alien compared to the skies of home, he thought. Stonehenge had been built as a place of worship and as an observatory to follow the northern stars, the stars of home on the ancient Salisbury Plain.

Suddenly the fog in his brain cleared. His heart lifted as he realised the truth. This was now home. This new Salisbury had its own stars, its own past and its own future. And he and his family would be part of that future.

'I name this brew *Spiritus Salisburyensis*,' he proclaimed, slurring the esses a little. 'God bless her and all who consume her.'

Twenty-five years passed, and the paddocks were gone. The Scotch thistles were extinct. The septic tanks had been supplanted by sewerage and smooth roads replaced the gravel that had served the area at first. Manicured lawns and well kept suburban houses filled the subdivision that had become a suburb. Trees flourished on the footpaths.

Fred had long since passed on, a victim of cirrhosis. Milly and Dot had forgiven their husbands their part in his demise, although the men had been banned from producing anything stronger than home brew beer.

Bill made his way down the hill to Charlie's house and opened the gate. He fielded the attentions of Charlie's blue heeler dog. The dog skittered off to lie in the shade under the big yellow wattle tree that paved Charlie's garden with gold. Bill walked around to the back of the house where a low, insistent rumbling, booming sound came from Charlie's shed, magnified by the corrugated iron.

'The banksias are looking real good, Charlie,' said Bill, entering the shed.

Charlie stopped playing his instrument. It was a length of PVC piping decorated with what looked vaguely like Aboriginal designs. He was sitting in a beanbag on the cement floor with a half-drunk stubby of beer beside him.

'That banksia's a bloody grevillea, Bill,' he responded. 'I keep telling you that. The bloody banksias are round the front. Get yourself a beer.'

Bill opened the fridge. The fridge door had a poster of Stonehenge stuck to it with little magnets. He reached in and took a stubby, then flopped down into the other beanbag, opened the beer and indicated the picture on the refrigerator door.

'New, is it?' he asked. 'The picture, not the fridge.'

'Young David sent it over. He's still in the UK on his working holiday. Don't know how he stands the bloody weather, though. He keeps whingeing about it every time he rings Milly up to send more Vegemite. I think he thought I might like to see that the old place is still standing. Are you going to have a practice on the didge?'

Bill picked up another length of PVC piping that lay next to his beanbag. 'Yair, in a minute. Wanted to have a bit of word first, though. You seen that Chinese bloke up the road a bit? The one who moved in a couple of weeks ago?'

Charlie nodded. 'Actually, I think he might be Vietnamese.'

'Whatever. Anyway, I was thinking we ought to get to know him. Seems a pity not to make him fit in, like. Besides, young Brett is pretty keen on his daughter, Kylie. Dot had the fellow's wife over for an aromatherapy party, but I reckon us blokes ought to do something. What do yer reckon?'

Charlie considered the idea. 'What did you have in mind?' he asked.

'Well,' said Bill. 'I was thinking of organising a European wasp hunt. All we need is a couple of tins of fly spray and maybe some fly swats and perhaps a picture of the buggers so we know what we're looking for. We can say they're a real threat to the neighbourhood. We'll get him interested in it, then we'll bring him back here and teach him to play the didgeridoo. We'll have to get another beanbag and another length of the old PVC, though.'

'That's a crazy idea, Bill,' said Charlie.

'Bunnings has got heaps of PVC,' protested Bill. 'And I reckon there's another old beanbag in my shed somewhere.'

'European wasps?' asked Charlie. 'I don't think he'll fall for that one.'

'I dunno. You fell for the trapdoor spiders, didn't you? We'll throw some chops on the barby and have a few beers afterwards. Get him into the neighbourhood culture, like. Pity we can't have a still again. The women would never stand for that, though. Do you remember that still, Charlie? Bloody good drop that was.'

'The memory lingers still,' said Charlie, picking up the PVC. 'We'll give it a go, Bill.'

'What did you call that stuff?'

'*Spiritus Salisburyensis*,' said Charlie, 'the Spirit of Salisbury.'

Nemesis

Brian O'Malley's the name, sixth-generation Australian. My granddad was on the Kokoda track, my great-grandfather fought at Gallipoli. But when I'm in a crowd of Greeks, I fit in like an olive tree in a grove. My fluent Greek is tinged with the accent of the island of Kos, I'm olive-skinned, although that's mainly from hours of working in the sun and sea, and around my neck I wear a heavy gold cross and a chain that once belonged to my brother, Nikkos.

Nikkos and I grew up in Port Lincoln, a little town on the west coast of South Australia where limestone hills surround a harbour with water blue as a tourist's dream of the Adriatic at one moment, wine-dark and stormy as Homer's seas the next; a place that needs only a ruined temple on a hilltop to evoke Greece. Tuna and wheat, that's Port Lincoln.

Nick and I were inseparable. His mother had trouble with my Celtic barbarian Aussie name, so I became Yiorgos, her second son. In Greek culture, traditionally, the first son, she told me, must be named after his paternal grandfather, hence Nikkos's Christian name. The second boy was given the name of the maternal grandfather. Her father's name had been Yiorgos. Nikkos quickly converted this to George, the English equivalent. Reborn, I accepted my new identity with enthusiasm. The noisy exuberance of my Greek family gave me far more pleasure than my true Aussie antecedents, whom I viewed as boring and staid.

Gradually, my biological mum came to terms with my breath reeking of garlic when I came back from spending time with Nick's family, but she refused to cook the squid that Nikkos and I caught off the jetty.

'That's bait for fishing, Brian, not fish for eating,' she protested, as she looked up briefly from scrubbing crumbs from the collecting tray of her toaster with an old toothbrush. 'I'm not having that smelly rubbish in my clean kitchen.'

Of course she was right: calamari did not belong in the sterile surroundings of our house.

After that, I took my share of our catch to Nick's home. We lads sat together on a wooden bench at a table under the grapevines at the back of his house while his mum loaded food onto our plates – savoury moussaka and dolmades, sweet and sticky baklava and *ravanni*, my favourite honey cake.

His dad and grandfather saluted us with retsina and drank the health of both their boys. They crowned us with wreaths woven from the trees in the garden – laurel leaves for the victories that life would surely bring us, and apple blossom to avert the wrath of Nemesis, who chastises hubris. Jokingly, they referred to us as Castor and Pollux, the heavenly twins.

We both called Nikkos's grandfather Pappou. Spellbound, we sat at his feet as he told us of the glories of ancient Greece, tales of gods and heroes, of battles and love, of man's striving to overcome fate and death. Pappou was our Homer, our link to immortality. His old eyes looked beyond us, beyond time itself. Through Pappou, we knew that we boys were one with Odysseus, with Achilles, with Agamemnon and with Alexander. We, too, would conquer the world.

Our battle for Troy was fought beside the family chicken coop. In the personas of Achilles and Patroclus, we imprisoned Nick's cousins, Helen and Cassandra, in the hen house and marched up and down brandishing our wooden swords. We yelled imprecations at the tearful Trojan princesses and the squawking chooks until Nick's mum seized our weapons and used them to hit us on our backsides. She banished us, shamefaced, to her kitchen where we joined the girls for milk and fragrant, freshly baked *kourabiedes* biscuits.

One hot morning, hidden in the shade beneath the Port Lincoln jetty, we swore an oath of brotherhood. We sliced our fingers with our filleting knives and joined the two wounds so that our blood flowed together. We vowed that nothing could or would ever separate us.

We dived off the jetty when Father Asterios, blessing the Greek fishing fleet, cast a golden cross into the ocean, and together we followed the cross as it spiralled down, shining like a beacon in the darkening water. My father said this was a old pagan custom invoking the ancient gods of Greece, and should not be tolerated in a Christian country, but I knew he was wrong. Was it not the symbol of Christ that we followed into the darkness? Could not the sign of Jesus dispel any hint of sorcery? And what did my father know? Although brought up in the Catholicism of his remote Irish ancestors, he was not a religious man; his was the culture of beer and pubs and racing pigeons. My Greek family was wiser. I knew where my preferences lay.

One year, Nikkos would rise triumphant holding the cross aloft; the next year, the glory was mine. Not another lad in Port Lincoln could dive like my brother Nikkos or me, not a boy in the town was our equal in the water.

We decided on the same career, marine archaeology. We planned to attend university in Adelaide, then come back to Port Lincoln and work on the tuna boats for a season to build up our funds and complete our PhDs to qualify for success. We would work locally for a season to increase our experience and our bank accounts, then we would depart for Greece, where the real action, the true archaeology, all the glory and the history of the past, lay beneath the sparkling sea. Our futures mapped precisely, we knew that our dreams would be realised and that we could and would decree our own fates.

In Adelaide, Nikkos and I shared a flat and expenses all through our university years. Sometimes we shared the same girls. No problems there; it was share and share alike. We were irresistible to them with our youth, our vigour and our charm. Usually when we visited bars, it was the girls who propositioned us. We were bronzed and glorious young gods.

But no girl could cope with Nick's sudden mood changes. Like the sea blown by the wind, he was one moment sunny, the next tempestuous. I was accustomed to him, but even though eventually I began to see him through other people's eyes, I always made allowances for his behaviour. He was my brother. Nothing mattered, girls were ephemeral, there were plenty of fish in the sea, we said. Those were good years; we played hard but we studied hard. Nick always did slightly better than I managed in our exams, but it was a matter of distinctions and high distinctions.

'What did you expect, Nick? The gods preferred you because of your Greek blood,' I said. 'That's why you topped the state.'

'The gods aren't that clever, George. I'm just naturally smarter than you are.'

The family summoned us to Port Lincoln for Pappou's funeral. The ceremony with its colour and its solemn chanting, at once doleful and magnificent, and the sharp scent of incense that Father Asterios wafted over the marble face of Pappou, silent and surrounded by flowers in his open coffin, brought us both to tears. We mourned our lost grandfather and knew our link to the past was severed.

I visited my own parents' house that weekend, more out of a sense of filial duty than for any other reason. Mum was busy with her quilting group and had little time to spend with me. Dad was at the pub, catching up with his friends in the pigeon racing club. After that, the weekly phone calls I had made to them became even less frequent.

University over, Nick and I looked for jobs. The government was funding study into the myriad shipwrecks that lay off South Australia. Little was known about these wrecks or their state of preservation and it was necessary to collect data before amateur divers despoiled them. There were two positions available. We got them.

Because, on paper at least, Nick had won more kudos, he would be the top man, and I his assistant at a slightly reduced pay. It meant nothing; we were brothers, what was his was mine, what was mine was his. Our first posting would be to work with shipwrecks off Eyre Peninsula. There were plenty of wrecks there from the 1850s, wooden vessels that had sunk before the lighthouses were built and mariners learned that those smiling waters could be treacherous.

'You see, George,' said Nikkos, 'success comes easily to us. This is not hubris. The gods do love us!'

We went home. We had a few weeks before our contract began and Uncle Stavros agreed to take us out on his boat. I had a new underwater camera, a grudging graduation gift from my parents, made after I mentioned on the phone that Nikkos's parents had presented him with expensive diving equipment, including a spear gun.

I should explain that this all happened before tuna were farmed in sad little ponds anchored in the sea, back when a man needed skill, muscle and endurance to harvest the tuna that brought prosperity to Port Lincoln.

The spotter planes had already found the schools of tuna by locating the vast dark clouds of pilchards in the sunlit water. Tuna are voracious hunters of pilchards. Herding the shoals together, they attack and feed in a frenzy. Then the other predators come, fishermen, dolphins, seals, and the great white shark. Port Lincoln is famous for its man-eating sharks.

We cast our long lines and hauled in the heavy tuna, jewel colours gleaming as the fish danced and died on the deck in the sun. When Uncle Stavros and his men took a break to ease their backs and to indulge in cigarettes and coffee, Nick and I donned our scuba gear to slip over the side into the wine dark sea.

'No!' thundered Nikkos's uncle. 'Remember the sharks!'

Ignoring his warning, we entered the water.

Nick pulled off his mask and grinned up at his uncle. 'They say you don't see sharks when there are dolphin about,' he said, 'and I saw a pod of dolphins following our wake earlier.'

'You shouldn't believe everything you hear,' bellowed Uncle Stavros, throwing his cigarette into the water in disgust. 'Maybe no one told the sharks that old story.'

We waved at him and dived deep. I wanted to photograph the biomass of fish. Nikkos intended to spear a tuna with his new spear gun. The pilchards, a wall of silver, rotated as one entity. The theory is that this tactic confuses the predators. Nick and I were confused, but the tuna were feeding well. A pod of dolphins and some seals had joined the feast and I suspected Uncle Stavros was right, the sharks were probably there too, lurking silent and invisible in the Stygian dark background.

I took photos rapidly, sensing a hidden menace, wanting to surface but unwilling to admit my fear. Nikkos, who wanted to try out his new spear gun, took aim at a large tuna and fired. Grinning at me behind his face mask, he gave me the victory sign.

With the curiosity of youth, a baby dolphin left its mother's side to inspect the human intruders into its world. Horrified, I watched as it swam into the path of the missile. We were powerless to prevent the inevitable.

The small body writhed, impaled on the spear. Nikkos dropped his gun, swam to the baby dolphin, clasped it to his body, headed for the surface. I reached the boat as, still clutching the limp corpse, he was pulled aboard by the fishermen.

Uncle Stavros seized the dead dolphin and pulled out the spear. Blood gushed from the wound, sprayed Nikkos's face mask and turned his black rubber suit scarlet.

Nick's uncle lifted the corpse high before casting it into the deep. For an instant, his figure and that of the dolphin's body were silhouetted against the blue sky. Then, as a cloud covered the sun, I felt the presence of wrathful Poseidon, of Zeus and all the gods of the sea and of the earth. I shivered in my wetsuit.

Cursing Nikkos, Stavros cast the carcase overboard. 'I should throw you after it, you damned fool!' he yelled at Nikkos, who, covered in the dolphin's blood, had slumped to his knees on the deck.

The mother dolphin rose to the surface, baring her teeth and clicking loudly at the fishermen who were clustered at the side of the vessel watching the small body sink slowly through the sunlit water. Accustomed to see joy on a dolphin's face, I was astounded at the creature's expression as she nudged her child's torn body towards the surface, displaying the crime that Nikkos had committed.

'You have brought the curse of Poseidon and of Nemesis on us all! Nemesis will never rest until you are destroyed!' shouted Uncle Stavros, shaking his fist at his nephew.

The fishermen made the sign against the evil eye. I shook my head, refusing to believe that in Australia, in this scientific era, grown men could be so superstitious. But I, too, had felt doom descending on this boat which now rocked wildly in an angry sea. I looked at Nikkos, who moaned, making the sign of the cross over his chest repeatedly.

'I can never enter the water again. Nemesis will follow me,' he sobbed.

I embraced him, removed his bloody mask, stroked his wet hair. 'It was an accident. It wasn't your fault. We'll confess to the priest and ask forgiveness.'

'There are no priests for the old gods any more, George. No one will forgive me. I'm cursed.'

Ashore, I headed for a jeweller and bought a gold cross and a chain. I took it to Father Asterios for his blessing.

To hedge my bets, I gathered dry wood from the apple tree sacred to Nemesis. I lit a small fire on the beach, not far from the massive Doric pillars of the silos. I wrung the neck of a white pigeon stolen from my father's coop, threw the limp body into the flames and watched the smoke ascend. I raised my hands in supplication and exhorted Nemesis, although part of me scoffed at my sacrifice.

'O vanquishing deity who turns the wheel of life,' I prayed, 'spare my brother. For I know you, Nemesis, to be a vengeful goddess, who watches unjust acts, chastising proud and disdainful ways.'

In a sudden fit of anger against my ridiculous behaviour, I kicked the embers of the fire. What if I'd been seen? What explanation could I give? And if one did have lingering faith in the supernatural, surely Christianity had dispelled the ancient gods?

I presented the cross and chain to Nikkos. Tomorrow our work of categorising wrecks would begin and he must be convinced that he would be safe in the sea.

He accepted the cross with a show of bravado. 'Did you really think I was afraid, George? Afraid of an ancient curse?' He laughed at me as he tossed his head, his mane of dark hair shining in the sun. 'But I will wear the cross because you ask me to, because we are brothers.'

I was relieved to see the outline of the cross under his scuba suit as we sat in a line, facing forward into the departmental boat above the wreck. As our leader, Nick would dive first. I would follow, then our assistants in order of seniority. We waited for the dive master's command to throw ourselves backwards into the sea.

'No one goes! No one goes!' screamed the dive master.

Perplexed, we gazed at him and then turned to look into the water. Below the boat cruised the biggest shark I have ever seen.

Pulling off his mask, Nikkos vomited into the sea. 'I'm out of here!' he announced. 'Nemesis is after me. You get the top job, George. I'm leaving town. I'm getting as far away from Port Lincoln as I can go.'

He phoned me from Darwin to say that he had found a job. The Northern Territory government was funding research into the wrecks of World War II vessels in Darwin harbour, both American and Australian ships bombed by the Japanese. There would be work for many divers there.

'And the curse?' I asked.

'Darwin's a long way from Port Lincoln,' he said. 'I'll be all right up here. Darwin's a great town. It's a whole different world up in the Top End, George. You ought to come up here too. Beer and frangipani, beautiful girls in skimpy clothes, tropical weather. People think you're stuck up if you wear shoes. Whole different outlook on life. No room for old superstitious ideas, everyone lives for today, not yesterday. And no one in Darwin thinks of tomorrow, either.'

He phoned a week later. His self-assurance had vanished. His voice shook. He had gone out to dive on a wreck in the harbour. The dive was aborted when a huge crocodile had silently surfaced beside the boat. He described the murky green waters, seemingly empty of life, then the arrival of the enormous reptile, revealing at first only its implacable amber eyes and then gradually its vast corrugated prehistoric body, while the dive master waved his arms and shrieked hysterically at the fear-frozen divers.

'I can't take the sea any longer. I'm going to Alice Springs. That's about as far from the water as you can get in Australia. She won't be able to follow me there.'

She, I knew, was Nemesis, ancient goddess of retribution. I was reminded of Oedipus, who fled his home to evade his fate and met it in a strange land. But I said nothing. Perhaps in Alice Springs he would be safe.

Nick was happy in Alice Springs. He bought a pizza shop in Todd Mall and had three men working for him. Unable to relinquish intellectual studies entirely, he spent his spare time on palaeontology trips with people from the local museum, digging up fossilised shark teeth from the blood-red sands of the ancient seabeds that once covered the Red Centre. His PhD more than qualified him for that, and they were a good crowd, the museum blokes, he said.

I worried about this news. Could Nemesis or the old gods of the sea reach him still in Central Australia, across the divide of time, culture and distance? I warned him not to scratch himself with his digging tools or with the fossils. I said that he might get an infection from those shark teeth, but he laughed and said I was becoming an old woman, worrying about nothing.

'The teeth are so bloody old and dry the sea has forgotten them. You've been around Greeks for too long, mate. Come up here and get real. We're having a regatta in the Todd. That's the local dry riverbed. Hardly ever gets water in it. Hasn't rained in the Alice for years. The regatta's held every year.'

'But what if it rains?' I interrupted him.

'Never happens,' he assured me. 'The blokes from the pizza shop and me have built a boat, looks like an ancient Greek trireme only it's got no bottom. You stand in it, hold the sides and run like hell. We've named her *Nemesis*. Good advertising for the shop too. There'll be red dust flying everywhere when we get going. We'll have a few beers. I'll show you around the Alice. It'll be like old times. Do you good, mate.'

'Nikkos, don't tempt her,' I shouted. 'Don't call the boat *Nemesis*, don't ask for trouble!'

'Bloody hell, George, stop yelling at me in Greek. We speak English up here. The fellows from the pizza shop'll think you're a bloody wog if you go on like that. This is Australia, this is the Alice. Forget the bullshit, ancient Greek curses don't work in the Red Centre. By the way, it's Nick up here, not Nikkos, and I reckon you'd better be Brian.'

I flew north. We shook hands at the airport. I wanted to embrace him in the Greek manner but I sensed it was no longer appropriate. I was relieved to see that he still wore the gold chain with the cross I had bought him. I hoped that it afforded him some protection from fate, from evil. He was excited about the regatta, but worried because rain had been predicted for the MacDonell Ranges, amongst which the town of Alice Springs lies.

'Only regatta in the world gets cancelled if there's water in the river,' he told me. 'It'd be a real pity if the authorities stopped it, if you missed seeing all the fun.'

He was developing an incipient beer gut, he had a couple of skin cancers beginning on his nose, and his hair was thinning. He wore thongs on his bare feet, a T-shirt inscribed with 'Nick's Pizza' and shorts. He had become a Territorian. I shook my head and smiled. Beneath the veneer, he was still my brother Nikkos.

Most of the Alice and I stood in the red dust beside the dry river course the next day. Nikkos in the *Nemesis* waved to me from the flotilla which waited at the starting line. He and his mates from the pizza shop had done well. The mock trireme's lines were classical and the high prow was painted with the blue eye which gave protection from the evil eye and from sea monsters. Along the side was painted 'Nick's Twenty-four-hour-a-day Pizza', which detracted only a little from the design.

The day was hot and still. Even I, a stranger to the place, felt that a storm loomed. Under dark clouds, the sweating spectators drank cold beer and shouted encouragement. The bed of the Todd River was dry and red dust rose beneath the restless feet of the crowd.

'No rain yet, mate. She's right,' said Nick.

The race would go ahead. The starting pistol was fired and the competitors began their sprint just as the first huge drops splashed into the sand.

There was a crackle from the speaker tower. 'Stop! No one goes. Get out of the riverbed!' I heard over the static. 'There's a flash flood coming.'

The race was abandoned, the boats dropped to the ground, their crews fled.

Alone, Nikkos, abandoned by his mates, clutched his bottomless boat. Did he disbelieve the announcement? I was having trouble coming to terms with it myself. Surely such a desiccated stream could not spring to life as quickly as this?

A trickle of brown lace appeared on the riverbed. It reminded me of the creamy topping on the cappuccino that we had had in the pizza shop that morning. Behind it came the merest little creek of muddy water, a rivulet that tumbled a few twigs and pebbles before it Innocuous, unthreatening. But the land and the spectators seemed to be holding their breath. Why did Nikkos not move? Why was he frozen like a mouse mesmerised by a cat?

'Nikkos, come away,' I called as the smell of moisture filled the air, the scent of water soaking into long parched earth, the stench of something menacing – unforeseen, unpredictable, impossible –approached.

I heard the water long before I saw it.

Suddenly the stream was knee-deep with swirling currents, but still Nikkos stood clutching the sides of his bottomless vessel. I shouted at him in English and in Greek to run. A tidal wave hit the *Nemesis*, hurled it high, then sent it crashing down. A tsunami that carried branches and then whole trees before it, tumbling in the flood water that was now dark brown, red as the soil of Central Australia, scarlet as arterial blood.

Nikkos was thrown clear. He was near the edge and I thought he would crawl out of the murderous water, would climb out and give himself a shake and come back to me, grinning and saying something like, 'Well, mate, she didn't get me that time.'

But then the prow of the *Nemesis*, turned by the brown water, lunged towards him and hit him on the temple. He sank beneath the muddy water and I flung myself into the river. I found him and held him and dragged him to the shore. There was no pulse. The blood from the wound on his head ran over my chest, as the dolphin's blood had stained him so long ago.

In grief and anger, I raised my hands to the sky. I shouted at the waters and at the goddess I knew had sent the rains. 'I take the blood and the guilt and the sin and the punishment on my shoulders. I am more Greek than he is now. Let him live, let me carry the burden for him.'

I felt him stir beneath my hands, heard a sigh as life and breath returned. I snatched the gold chain and cross from him and put it around my neck. Perhaps she had recognised him because he wore that cross.

'I only lent it to you, Nick.' I said, as he regained consciousness.

'I should have known it,' he said. 'Beware of Greeks bearing gifts, as the Trojans said.'

Nick makes pizza in Alice Springs. He no longer seeks sharks' teeth. He plays football or drinks beer in his spare time. He reminds me a lot of my father and I keep expecting him to tell me he has taken up racing pigeons.

I'm a marine archaeologist and I spend most of my time in the sea. I wear Nick's gold cross and chain although I know it cannot protect me against Nemesis. Nothing can. As Nick once said, there are no priests for the old gods. I used to look over my shoulders all the time, but I don't any longer. She knows where I am. She will come when she is ready.

The Holiday of a Lifetime

'Anything to declare?' asked the Customs man. It was good to hear an Australian accent again.

'Only,' said Sally, clutching her bag containing her change of underwear, some biscuits in case she was hungry, a Mills and Boon novel, and a tin labelled English Lavender Talc, 'that I've had the holiday of a lifetime.'

That was what John had planned; he had said they would never have another chance to go, and they must make the best of it, even if her knees were playing up and his heart was a bit funny.

She remembered his exact words. 'If we don't go now, Ducks, we never will. Bit like that ad for the Territory – "If you never, never go, you'll never never know."'

'But we know all about England, love,' Sally had protested. 'That's where we're from, both of us, even though we've lived here all these years. We ought to have a look at the Continent while we're there, too. We never had the money to go over before when we lived there, so now we've got a bit put by we might as well do that too. See Italy and France and maybe even Spain. All the young ones do it, why shouldn't we? Not just see the same old England. We need something a bit different to spice things up, like.'

John said that it wouldn't be the same old England they knew that they were going back to, it was thirty years since they'd left. It would be a totally different England now.

'There'll always be an England,' sang Sally.

John shook his head. 'You mark my words, it'll all be changed. You can't expect it to stand still, Ducks. Things have changed here in thirty years, stands to reason they've changed there too. But I hope Kensington Park is still the same. I remember as a lad playing with my little boat in the Round Pond in the park. Best days of my life. We have to go back there, Sal.'

Sally sighed. She had set her heart on lunch in a little bistro in Paris, not an expensive one, just one a bit off the Champs Elysées, where she had heard prices were a bit lower. She had been reading all the travel pages in *The Advertiser* for months, and planning how to spend their time and their money.

'Still, since you want to see Europe, we could do a tour and then fly back to Australia from Rome. It'd probably only add a thousand or two to the cost – yes, why not? It's our chance for a real holiday. Trip of a lifetime, so to speak.'

It turned out to cost more than John's estimated thousand or two. Still, what was money for? Life was short, and their son didn't need it, he was doing all right. Only, what would Peter say when she broke the news to him?

'Oh, I have got something to declare,' she said to the customs man. 'I've got a bottle of Southern Comfort that I just got in that liquor store over there. It's for my son Peter. He's probably going to need it.'

The plane trip over had been lovely. The air hostesses were so nice and brought food and drinks and they had watched movies and then on the screen John had watched which countries they were flying over, and Sally had watched the towering clouds outside the window. It was all a dream come true. She had got up and walked around just as the doctor said she should. Kept the joints moving. John said he felt fine.

The jet lag hadn't been all that bad either. London was bigger and cleaner and noisier than they remembered. Lots of new buildings. And foreigners. That big green glass Gerkin building was a shock, although they decided they liked it, and there was a new bridge over the Thames people called the Wibbly-Wobbly. But the Tube was much the same, and the Embankment and the Thames and St Pauls were still there.

One of the first things they had done was to visit Kensington Park. John was so happy. Nothing much was changed there. The sun was actually shining, and kiddies were still running about and playing with little boats on the pond. Same trees, same ducks – or they looked the same ducks. Generations later, though, they agreed.

On the third day, John said he felt a bit queer, and the Anginine didn't seem to help much. The people in the hotel were very good.

They called an ambulance and John and Sally were taken to a big new hospital.

'If the worst comes to the worst,' said John, 'you get me cremated here and go on with the trip. We're not going to waste all that money and not get value for it.'

'I can't do that, John,' wept Sally, 'and you can't die, you can't go and leave me here on my own. What would Peter say, anyway?'

'No need to tell Peter anything until you get back home. He'd only get upset.'

Sally tearfully protested but John was adamant. He wanted to be cremated and he wanted his ashes scattered in Kensington Park.

'He must have known,' Sally told the ducks, 'and that's why he wanted to come back now. He never was one to waste money. Not tight, mind you, just careful. So I'll have to do what he wanted, won't I? Don't know how I'm going to manage with all them foreigners, though, and me a new widow and on my own. And I've got to leave his ashes here as well. Tell you what, I'll scatter most of him here and just keep a bit of him to keep me company.'

She was a little dismayed when one of the flock scooped up some of John's ashes in its bill and swallowed him with apparent relish. 'Can't blame it, though. Make a change from bread,' she thought. And after all, he had always called her Ducks, hadn't he? Maybe it was his fate, like.

The tour people were very nice, very understanding. She even got a refund on John's fare. She put his ashes in an empty English Lavender Talc tin and packed it carefully in her suitcase under her knickers. 'He'd have been right chuffed. It would have pleased him, that would,' Sally thought. 'All right, John, we're off on our grand tour of Europe.'

She took him everywhere with her, up the Eiffel Tower, on a cruise on the Rhine, to the Colosseum and the Swiss Alps. She made sure the talc tin was in her day bag so John wouldn't miss out on any of the sights. She could afford to go a bit further, stay a bit longer, now that there was only one of her to pay for. Of course, there was that single increment thing, but it was still cheaper than two fares.

She phoned Peter and said they had decided to add the Greek islands and Turkey to their itinerary. He asked after Dad, and she said he was keeping very well. He fitted nicely into the talc container, but she didn't say that to Peter.

'Your bottle of Southern Comfort's fine, love,' said the customs man. 'You're allowed to bring in two litres of alcohol. No worries, not a problem in the world.'

'Thanks, love,' said Sally, 'It's nice to have no worries. S'pose I might have a few now I'm back home, but it's been worth it. Everyone deserves a holiday of lifetime once at least in their life.'

Sangue di Terra

In the fading light, Nick sits in his small stone cottage overlooking the ghost of the vineyard he had once loved. The cottage smells of musty books and wine and despair. Old books and old memories surround him. He gazes into the glass of wine before him. Red wine, red as the earth from which it came, red as the blood that flowed on the earth. Blood, wine and earth.

He knows the ancient stories of Dionysus and the old gods and sacrifice in the vineyards were best left in the old world, but he has resurrected them here, and now he will never be free of them. He hears voices among the vines. Are those voices cursing, or whimpering in pain, or do they mutter endearments? He cannot quite hear, but he is aware of their presence, and, awake or asleep, they haunt his mind.

'Blood of the earth,' he murmurs, raising the glass to his lips.

The doctor has warned him that his liver will kill him unless he curbs his drinking. His cirrhosis is advanced. Death from cirrhosis, he knows, means drifting into a coma from which he will not awake. It sounds a pleasant death, and a release from his present torment. Will the voices follow him into that coma…will he hear them still in death? He would leave if he could, but where could he go where they would not follow? His roots are in this earth. His life, his blood, are tied to this place, to this red soil.

'Blood of the earth,' he repeats, the wine bringing back memories of vintages past.

Once, from the stone cottage, he looked out joyfully on a sea of vines that tossed in the wind or drooped under the hot sun and the weight of their fruit, or held bare arms aloft for pruning under the cold grey skies of winter. The old man knew and loved those vines. He had never married, had never felt the need to love a woman, but he would walk in the evenings along the green rows, caressing, touching the leaves, feeling their leathery veined texture, cradling the heavy bunches of grapes in his callused hands, smelling the acrid scent of the unborn wine.

Then back to his cottage, where he would read into the night. Homer and his wine-dark sea, the tragedies and comedies of ancient Greece, the myths and legends of the Mediterranean. He prided himself on his Greek heritage under the Australian sky, and saw his life as a labourer in the vineyard of life. These were his obsessions, hard work and solitude and study. He desired nothing more.

The boss used to say that Nick Petros was the best worker he had ever had. Nick was always the first out there in the morning no matter how frosty it was, pruning and carting away the cuttings and checking the young grapes, and then at vintage driving the tractor which drew the dray on which sat the pickers with their buckets in the bright, cool mornings when the chorus of magpies shouted alleluias and the vineyard smelled fresh with the sharp acrid tang of the leaves before, later in the day, the heat descended to wilt labourers and vines.

'The '96, that was a vintage,' says Nick as he raises the glass again. He studies the light shining through the dark wine, sniffs at the liquid, and tastes it. 'The best wine was saved for the last.'

The '96. A late vintage. The summer had been dry and the sugar content rose as the grapes ripened in the hot sun. The rows between the vines were ploughed to drive snakes out, and so that the weeds would not impede the slow progress of the pickers. This vineyard had old vines, unsuitable for the new machines. Nick hated machines. Old ways were the best ways. Here, human hands would clip the bunches and toss them into the yellow plastic buckets and men would lift the buckets and heave them into the great bin sitting on the dray drawn by Nick's tractor.

Nick took the pickers out in the bright morning. There were the regulars, the people he knew who came each year to help with the pruning and then for the harvest. There was his offsider, Joe the Italian, who would stand behind Nick on the tractor, watch for the full buckets, leap off and toss the bucket into the bin all in one swift movement, while never missing the chance to look up the skirt of any female foolish enough not to wear trousers. Old May, who despite her obesity could work as well as any man, and her friend the thin Scotswoman, Lizzie, greeted him.

'What sort of workers have we got this year, Nick?' asked May.

'Dunno,' said Nick. 'S'pose we'll know by the end of the day. One day in the sun usually sorts them out.'

'Don't think they'll last it out,' said Lizzie, surveying the crew climbing onto the dray. 'Lot of housewives, not used to real work. A few blokes on the dole. But what the hell are they doing here?' She indicated a couple sitting together on the back of the dray, legs swinging as though they were off on a picnic.

The girl was young, blonde, beautiful, and dressed in a skimpy top and pair of shorts. No hat covered the golden hair which flowed to her shoulders. The lad was equally glorious, tanned and well muscled and briefly clad.

'Looks like the bloody owners are making a documentary about grape picking,' said May. 'They don't belong out here – didn't anyone tell them what it's like? They'll be like lobsters by lunch break.'

'They're a couple of backpackers the boss put on,' said Nick. 'I'm only the bloody foreman, May. I can't say who works and who doesn't. As long as they do their share, that's all that matters. They don't speak much English, though, so it's going to be a bit hard. They come from Denmark or Norway, somewhere like that. Working their way around Australia, they are. Got work permits.'

After a couple of lessons from May in how to hold the secateurs, the young couple turned out to be surprisingly good workers. They were picking Grenache grapes, and the 'twins' as the older workers christened the couple, burrowed into the bushes and cut the gleaming purple grapes and filled the big buckets so that even Joe had trouble keeping up with them.

'Stop looking at the kid's legs, Joe,' ordered Nick, 'and put your bloody back into it.'

Joe shook his head, the sweat running off his brow beneath the wide brimmed hat he wore and down onto his black moustache. 'If you're going to bring distractions like that into the vineyard, Nick, you got to expect the workers to slow down a bit!' he replied.

There was a distraction in mid-morning when a brown snake slithered out of the bushes towards a woman with a floral apron over her jeans. She shrieked and ran, knocking over the pail of grapes. Joe swore and gathered up the fruit as the woman ran away in the direction of the gate.

'That's one less!' said May grimly. 'Around twenty to go, I reckon. Worried about a snake…of course, the black snakes are bad, the brown ones are worse, but the trouser snakes are the worst of all. If they get you, you swell up something awful. What colour was that one, Nick?'

'Dunno, didn't get a real good look at it,' said Nick. 'How about some work so we can fill this bin before lunch?'

The bin was filled, and the labourers ate their lunch, some lying under the dray, some under the vines. The twins disappeared, and after a while Nick, concerned that they were lost, went in search of them.

He found them when he saw a slim golden ankle protruding from under a large grapevine which shook violently. He heard low, ecstatic moans in a Scandinavian language. He stayed a moment, shook his head, then made his way back to the gang sprawled on the lumpy red earth.

'Them twins aren't twins,' he announced. 'Not unless they've got some funny ways in Denmark.'

Contrary to May's prediction, the couple did not look like lobsters by lunchtime, and over the weeks that followed, they grew honey-coloured and seemed to glow as they worked. The dust that stuck to the sweat and grape juice on the other labourers enhanced the young Danes' beauty as if the earth itself were in love with them. Each day at lunch break they would disappear hand in hand into the vineyard, and the others would smile and shake their heads, and Joe would croon an Italian love song as they left.

'I worry about them kids,' said May one day as the smiling couple left the group for their lovemaking under the sun. 'Rotten things happen to backpackers – they always seem to get murdered or beaten up. I'd hate anything nasty to happen to young Ingrid and Lars.'

'Anyone touches a hair of those kids' heads answers to me,' said Nick. 'I'm responsible for the gang in this vineyard and nothing nasty happens here.'

'I don't mean here,' said May. 'You'll look after them while they're here, Nick, but what happens when they leave? They're planning to work their way around Australia. You can't look after them then.'

Nick shook his head. He could not believe that anyone or anything could harm those golden children.

Halfway through the vintage, Nick had a message that the owner wanted to see him. Nick was hesitant to enter the quadrangle of winery buildings. He didn't mind the great vats where the grapes were dumped or even the crushing vats and the huge barrels where the wine sat maturing. He felt at home there. He often paused to peer into the vats and gaze at the purple juice that, given time and the correct temperature, would change to wine. A few leaves still floated on the surface, as if the vineyard clung to its child, unwilling to let it go. The vineyard smells hung to this place; life grew and fermented here. And he respected the vintners, the men who wrought the miracle of transmutation of juice to wine, even though much of their alchemy took place in gleaming laboratories these days.

But the offices, those air-conditioned deserts where nothing was produced but paper, where double-glazed windows kept out the scent and sounds of production, where human voices were muted and hesitant, and the hum of the computer replaced the laughter of the pickers and the sound of bees, that was an alien world to him.

Conscious of his dirty overalls and boots, Nick picked his way past the young well-dressed receptionists and secretaries and clerks and found the boss's office. He knocked hesitantly and entered when summoned. He took off his battered felt hat and apologised for his lack of cleanliness. He had come as soon as he was told he was wanted and had not had time to clean up.

'Sit down, Nick,' said the boss. 'No, it's all right, it's a leather chair, some one can wipe it over. I've got something to tell you, and I wanted to let you know before you hear it on the grapevine, so to speak.'

Nick smiled dutifully at the boss's attempt at humour, but the smile left his face as the boss continued.

'You've worked here a long time, Nick, and there'll always be a job for you somewhere on the property. We will find something for you to do. The point is, we've decided to pull out the old vines and put in new varieties. And the new vines will be set up for mechanical picking. So this will be the last vintage in the old style. It's just not economic to run the vintage manually any more.'

Nick knew the boss was talking. The boss's lips were moving, and there was sound of some sort in the room. There was definitely a buzzing in his ears but nothing that made any sense. Perhaps the crushing feeling in his chest stopped him from deciphering speech. Somehow he smiled, shook hands with the boss. As he stumbled from the office, he saw the boss wiping his hands surreptitiously on a tissue from a box on his desk.

That night, Nick carried an armful of bottles into the vineyard and sat beneath the vines in the moonlight. His heart felt black and dead. The darkness in his soul was darker than the darkness of the night. He crumbled a handful of earth and let the soil run between his fingers. In ancient Greece, a sacrifice to the gods would be called for at at time like this. In Greece, this could not have happened – the punishment for destroying an olive tree under Solon's law was death, he remembered. What was the punishment for destroying a vineyard? He could recall none – no one would dare think of destroying a vineyard.

He poured wine. A glass for himself, a glass for Dionysus. He tipped the libation carefully into the clods of earth.

'You can't let this happen, Dionysus,' he said. 'If you are a god, if you still exist, you have to stop it. What do you want? I'll give you anything you want, just don't let them destroy my world.'

Nick did not feel the night pass. Night had become part of his being and only the crowing of the cocks in the nearby farms alerted him to the dawn. He came to consciousness with his head throbbing. He struggled back to his cottage, swallowed bread and more wine, splashed cold water on his face, and mounted his tractor.

The serene vines, unaware of their fate, waved leafy arms and the magpies swooped and carolled as the pickers climbed on the dray laughing and chatting.

'What's up with Nick, May?' asked Lizzie. 'He looks like death warmed up.'

'Dunno.' said May. 'Maybe he's got the male menopause. Been hitting the bottle again, if you ask me. Smells of it, among other things. Hasn't had a shower. S'pose you want me to ask him?'

'Well, you and Joe have known him longer than anyone. Except maybe them old Greeks he's always on about.'

May shrugged. The ancient Greeks wouldn't be communicating with Nick, she knew that much.

'What's wrong with you, Nick?' asked May.

'Just got a headache, that's all,' said Nick. 'Let's get this crop picked, shall we? If we don't get it in on time, they might get machines in and you'll all be out of a job.'

The day wore on and at lunchtime the young Danes disappeared as usual. After the break, Nick stood up wearily and counted the pickers. He saw that once again they had not returned. 'Bloody kids. A man can't rely on labourers any more. Haven't they got watches? Don't they teach kids in Denmark any responsibility?'

Joe shrugged, and May sighed and said that sometimes work had to give way to better things.

'Reckon we'll just have to do without them for a bit,' said Nick. 'I'm not wasting time looking for them. They'll catch up later. I'll see that they do their share when they do get back, though.'

The bin filled. Somnolent, heavy bees crawled over the grapes. Still the lovers had not returned. Nick was irritated. He told Joe to stack the buckets at the end of the row. He would take the bin in and collect another and they would empty the buckets afterwards. He would look for the Danes on his way back to the winery.

'Bloody kids,' Nick said to himself as he drove the tractor down the row and rounded the fence post at the end heading for the track that led to the winery.

He was driving faster than usual. He was annoyed at those backpackers. Abusing privileges he should not have given them. He shouldn't have been so soft on them, he told himself. As if things weren't bad enough already.

He heard a loud metallic snap, then a grinding, crunching sound. 'Christ!' he shouted as the huge white bin, filled to the brim with purple grapes, left the dray. The bins were always secured with heavy cable. Surely the cable had not broken?

The bin fell towards the earth, spilling its load of grapes as it went, the angry bees, awoken from their drowsy feast, catapulted off in all directions. A tonne of grapes and the heavy iron bin crushed the vines as the container landed on its side. Purple grape juice ran into the parched earth.

Joe, who had heard the crashing sound and Nick's shouts, came running.

'Look at the bloody vines,' moaned Nick. 'They're ruined, crushed, finished.'

Joe, kneeling beside the upturned bin, was looking at what Nick had supposed to be grape juice, flowing in streams, forming little curving tendrils and soaking into the earth. '*Sangue*,' he whispered, '*sangue*.'

Then Nick realised that the fluid that was coming from under the bin, coagulating in long ropy ribbons, crimson against the green of the crushed leaves, smelled not of fermentation but of blood. And from under the bin protruded a slender ankle.

The coroner found no fault on the part of the foreman or of the vineyard owners. He called it death by misadventure – an act of God. Nick knew which god it was – Dionysus, god of the vine, who demanded human sacrifice for his bounty. He had read how the maenads, maddened by lust and wine, tore the bodies of the young apart with their bare hands to placate Dionysus, in return for a bountiful harvest. Yes, it was Dionysus, and Nick as his invoker, who had wrought sacrifice in this antipodean vineyard. Nick had awoken the old god, calling on him to save the vineyard, promising anything in order to avert fate. And the promised sacrifice had been made. Two young people had died, betrayed by one who had had them in his care. Betrayed by life, betrayed by all the gods – what after all, was an act of God?

'I didn't mean it!' he cried aloud in the vineyard in the moonlight. 'I didn't want you to take them like that. Why didn't you take me? I'm old and useless and broken and they were young and beautiful, full of hope and life. You were wrong to take them. And it won't help, because the boss is still going to destroy the vineyard. You are not a god, Dionysus. You are a devil.'

The old vines are gone now, replaced with vines that will accommodate the mechanical picker. The vines below Nick's cottage are young. Nick will never see them bear fruit. He sits in the shadows in the little cottage on the hill, and gazes into the dark glass. The wine clots and turns to blood in his mouth. He remembers how the old vines were ripped from the earth and lay up-ended, ravaged, red soil running from their naked roots in the rain, their life essence bleeding away. He remembers their twisted, knotted, ancient trunks, their branches held up in vain supplication to the grey heavens which wept as Nick too, wept.

The vines had outlived their usefulness, the owner said. Their day was over. Modern times dictate new tastes. The culture of wine had changed. The future demanded new varieties.

Nick has outlived his usefulness too. He raises his glass in salutation to his fate, and sips the dark wine in the night. He knows he is the next prey, for Dionysus, the god of the vines, lives and demands sacrifice. Soon Nick will hear the voices in the leaves again, and soon it will be his name they call.

Reading Between the Lines

'I wanna bust, I wanna gool, I wanna wead!' shrieked David from his pusher.

Katy's son, Michael, also in a pusher, sucked his thumb and watched David suspiciously.

'David's English is worse than my Number Six Auntie's English,' said Katy.

We watched as my daughter, Jacky, guided Katy's son Robert up the steps of the school bus and showed the driver their tickets. Robert turned to wave goodbye to us. Jacky wouldn't do that any more. Now that she was eleven, she needed to look grown up and independent. I sighed. It was hard to let my little girl grow up. At least David was still only three-and-a-half. Still a baby, really, even if he did have ambitions to read.

'David means that he wants to go on the bus, he wants to go to school and he wants to read,' I translated. 'I've dug up some old Dr Seuss books Jacky used to love. I thought I'd start teaching him to read. You know what I always say: you're never too young or too old to learn to read. It might keep him quiet for a while. You must get sick of hearing him yelling all day. Our houses aren't that far apart.'

'Actually, I will almost miss hearing him, now that I am going back to work. Trevor said I must return to the restaurant. He said it is difficult to get good staff and it would be good for me to get out of the house.'

'But Ulrich has only been dead for three months,' I gasped.

I bit my lip. I didn't like to remind Katy of her husband's death. It had been awful for all of us, watching as he slowly wasted away from cancer. Much worse for him, of course, and terrible for Katy and the children. Everyone admired Katy's courage. But I knew that if Trevor said Katy must go back to work, she would return to work. A Chinese woman did not argue with the head of her family, and Trevor was the head of Katy's family, now that Ulrich was dead.

'What about the boys?' I asked. 'Would you like me to look after them while you are at work?'

'No, Trevor has decided that Number Six Auntie will come and live with me and she will look after the boys. She will have Robert's room and Robert and Michael will share a room. Trevor said it will be company for me too, that I will not be alone at night. And of course, the boys will learn to speak Cantonese, which might be useful when they are older. I will bring food back from the restaurant, so my living expenses will be less. Auntie will also cook and clean. So, all round, it is a very good arrangement.'

I burst into tears and Katy hugged me.

'Everything will be all right,' she said.

'Sorry, I just think it's too soon, after all you've been through,' I sobbed. 'And I'll miss our coffee mornings. I'll hardly ever see you.'

'I am not leaving Valley View, Elizabeth,' Katy said. 'I will still be your next-door neighbour. I just won't be here all the time. I will be part-time at home, and part-time in the Scarlet Dragon. We will still be friends. And you can also be friends with Number Six Auntie. When she has cleaned my house, she will clean your house. She likes cleaning houses.'

'I'm not asking an old lady to clean my house. Anyway, what is her name? I don't know if I've I met her before,' I said, blowing my nose. 'You've got so many aunties, so I don't know which one she is. I can't say "Hello, Number Six Auntie," can I? She must have a name.'

'Her name is Hing, which means pretty, but all the family call her Number Six Auntie. There were six daughters and four sons in my grandfather's family. Because Hing was daughter number six, my grandfather said she should remain unmarried. He did not wish to pay dowry for another girl. And he said, it would always be useful to have a woman who would be a full-time auntie. Every family has a child who needs to be cared for, or an invalid who requires nursing.'

She bent to help me push David back into his pusher while her more docile son looked on placidly. She straightened up and shrugged. 'So that has been Number Six Auntie's life's work. She would have come to help me with Ulrich, but my brother in Sydney had need of Auntie when his wife broke her arm getting off the ferry. Auntie had to look after their children and do their cooking and cleaning for three months. And Trevor knew that I had you to help me, so I was all right and Number Six Auntie could stay in Sydney.'

I paused from adjusting David's restraints. He had managed to undo a couple of the straps and I didn't want him escaping and running down the street with me in pursuit as he'd done yesterday.

I opened my mouth, but before I could say what I was thinking, Katy interjected. 'Don't look at me like that, Elizabeth. That is the role of the unmarried auntie in our culture. Number Six Auntie doesn't know any different, she never complains. I believe she is content with her life, even proud of what she does. She knows she is making an important contribution to the family.'

'I haven't met her yet, Katy, but I still think it is sad that she didn't have a chance to make a life for herself, to have children of her own. I think your grandfather was cruel to control her like that.'

'But she has had a life, Elizabeth. She is always needed by someone in the family. If she had married, it would have been an arranged marriage and she might not have loved or even liked her husband. He might have beaten her if she displeased him. At least Hing did not die in infancy as many girl children at that time died. She is such a happy person. I know you will like her. She does not look downtrodden. Because she never married, she has a sort of independence and also a kind of dignity all of her own. Believe me, you will love her. Everyone does.'

And Katy was right. My children and I fell under Sixth Auntie's spell as soon as we met her.

Auntie came bearing gifts. I was amazed how little she was, smaller and slimmer even than Katy, who always reminded me of a tiny Oriental doll. Although Katy had told me that Auntie was almost seventy years old, her face was smooth and unlined, although her once-dark hair was mainly grey with only a few black streaks. I decided the word that best described her was serene.

'She's not pretty, Katy,' I said, looking over Sixth Auntie's shoulder at my friend. 'She is beautiful.'

'Sixth Auntie has made *bao*,' said Katy. 'She has brought some for you and for the children. She hopes that you will enjoy them.'

'Good boy,' said Sixth Auntie, patting David's head as I thanked her for the pork buns. David hugged Auntie's legs, which was unusual for him. He often took time to feel at ease with strangers.

'So you do speak English!' I said, smiling at her.

'That's about as much English as Sixth Auntie knows,' said Katy.

She said something in Cantonese to the old lady, and Sixth Auntie smiled at me and bent her head. I bent my head back at her.

'Thank you very much for the *bao*, Auntie Hing,' I said.

I was rewarded by an even bigger smile. I could not resist hugging her, although I was not sure if that was correct Chinese etiquette. But she smiled and hugged me back. I knew then that Auntie Hing and I were destined to become great friends.

After Katy was resumed her work in her brother's restaurant, Sixth Auntie and I walked the children to the bus each morning. I decided I would teach Auntie English, and began by pointing to objects in the street, naming them, and encouraging her to say the word after me. Soon she knew the words for tree, dog, cat, house, sky. I elaborated on that by adding colours – blue sky, green leaf, red dress.

One day I found a Chinese magazine in a shop and bought it for Auntie. I was so excited that I phoned Katy at the restaurant. 'I've got a magazine for Auntie,' I said. 'I'm going to take it over to her this afternoon when we go to get the kids from the bus.'

'No, Elizabeth,' said Katy urgently. 'You must not do that. She would be embarrassed. It would upset her dreadfully.'

'But she must want to read something. You know what I'm like, Katy, I couldn't bear to live without something to read. I even read the backs of cornflake packets if I haven't got anything else on hand. You like reading too. But you don't seem to have any Chinese books in your house. Auntie must miss reading. The lady in the shop said the magazine was in Cantonese, not Mandarin, so I thought Auntie would like it.'

'No, Elizabeth. Grandfather did not approve of girls being educated. Sixth Auntie has never learned to read. Grandfather said it was a waste to teach her because her destiny was to care for family members, not to work outside the house. So if you take a magazine to her, she will lose face because she will have to admit that she cannot read. Once I saw her pick up a Chinese newspaper and she held it upside down because she did not know which side was up. I laughed at her, and she began to cry. I didn't know she was illiterate until then, because she is very careful to hide it.'

I was appalled. How could anyone not read? I could not imagine life without books. In fact, my bibliophilia was the main source of conflict between me and my husband, Frank. He called it bibliomania. Our shelves were full, and still I brought books home. I still do; I hide them under my bed, in the back of the wardrobe, all over the house. I am addicted to books.

'Auntie has had the most awful life,' I told my husband. 'She can't read. She's been treated as a servant all her life. Katy says her grandfather nearly didn't allow her mother to keep her when she was born because they already had so many children. It was only because she was such a pretty baby that she was allowed to live at all. That's why they named her Hing. It means pretty.'

Frank looked up from his newspaper and shook his head. 'We don't know how lucky we are to live in Australia.'

'But that's not all. Katy said there was a massacre in Nanking back in 1937. The Japanese invaded Manchuria and renamed it Manchukuo. Aunty was four years old then, but she still remembers the dead people lying in the streets. The Japanese killed all the Chinese they could find. Apparently 300,000 Chinese people were murdered. Women and little girls were raped. It must have been horrible. It's a miracle that any of them escaped.'

'It's a miracle that she's not stark staring mad. She's such a nice, gentle lady.'

'I know,' I said. 'Aunty has carried that burden with her. And she's gone all her life without being able to read a book. If she could read, maybe she could escape that nightmare into a fantasy world occasionally. Quite apart from the fact that she'd be more independent, able to fill in her own Medicare forms, all that sort of thing. I know I'd hate to be dependent on people for stuff like that.'

'Why don't you teach her to read?' asked Frank.

He looked at David, who was sitting on the floor turning the pages of *The Cat in the Hat* and saying the words on the page. I still wasn't sure if the kid was remembering the words I had said were written there, or if he was actually reading the text. But it was keeping David quiet, and he believed he was 'weading'.

'You taught David to read,' he added. 'In fact, the silence is deafening.'

'I can't teach Auntie to read Cantonese,' I protested. 'I don't speak Chinese at all.'

'No,' said Frank patiently. 'But you have taught her to speak quite a bit of English. This morning when I was going out to get the paper, she said, "Hello, Fwank, how are you this lovely morning?" I was surprised, but I said, "Fine, Auntie, and how are you?" and she answered, "I am very well, thank you, and it is a nice day." She couldn't have carried on a conversation like that a few months ago. If you can teach her English, I don't see why you can't teach her to read. You could start with something simple like *The Cat in the Hat* and work up to more complicated stuff.'

'I'll have to be careful, though,' I mused. 'I don't want her to know that I know she can't read, and I don't want to insult her or make her "lose face" as Katy put it.'

'How will you do it?' Frank asked. 'Will you teach her the alphabet? That would be pretty complicated, wouldn't it, for a lady her age, coming from a different culture?'

'No, I think I'll use the same method I used on David. I'll teach her to sight read words, then I'll hope that she realises that words are made up of letters, and when she does, then I'll show her how letters can be used to form words. It seems to have worked on David, and he didn't have any culture at all, did he?'

'No, I think we all agree that David is completely without culture,' said Frank. 'Although he has mellowed since he discovered books.'

I asked Auntie to teach me to make *bao*. I took David along with me, and a supply of Dr Seuss books: *The Cat in the Hat, Green Eggs and Ham*, that sort of thing. I installed David and little Michael on the floor on a mat with the books and told David to read to Michael while we worked. I thought it might give Auntie a taste for literature to see the boys enjoy reading.

Auntie worked quickly, mixing the flour and water for the *bao* dough using chopsticks, which always astounded me. Even though Katy had showed me countless times, I was still hopeless at using the implements to eat with, let alone to cook.

'I'm a barbarian,' I told Auntie. 'I'll never get the hang of this.'

'I do not know what barb…whatever you said is, Elizabeth, but I know you a good woman,' said Auntie. 'And David is good boy. He can read.'

'Reading is easy,' I said. 'Look, this is an easy book. You could read it.'

'No, I cannot speak English, I cannot read a book in English. I am too old and stupid.'

'Auntie, you speak English. You're speaking English now. And you're never too old to learn to read. And you're not stupid.'

She began to laugh. 'But I had forgotten that we were not speaking Cantonese! I am speaking English now. You have changed my life, Elizabeth.'

'So let's change it a bit more. See, this is a cat. This is a hat. That word is CAT. That word is HAT.'

'That is a cat?' asked Auntie. 'That is funny cat. Cats do not wear hats, Elizabeth.'

'Yes, it's a picture of a cat for children. It's a cartoon cat. And that is a picture of hat on the cat's head. This is the word for cat. And this is the word for hat. This sentence is written, "The Cat in the Hat".'

Auntie put down the chopsticks, dusted her hands and examined the page carefully. 'This is the Cat in the Hat,' she said.

I could see that she was intrigued. I turned the page and read the words to her, pointing to them, and then showing her how the words illustrated the picture beside it.

She took the book from my hands and turned the pages reverently. 'I would like to read this book,' Auntie said. 'Elizabeth, you will please to show me how to do this thing? I would be very happy to read books. I am ashamed and sad that I never learnt how to do it. I have always felt that others are smarter than I am because I cannot read.'

'I know how you feel, Auntie,' I said. 'I always feel dreadful when I go to Trevor's restaurant and I can't hold the chopsticks properly. I would be honoured to show you how to read. But first would you please teach me how to manage the chopsticks correctly? Last time, I made a mess on the tablecloth and I was very embarrassed.'

Auntie smiled.

I never did learn how to make *bao* using chopsticks, although I managed to make them using a fork. David said they were OK, but not as good as the ones Auntie made, although Auntie praised my efforts.

But Auntie learned to read, at first *The Cat in the Hat*, then *Green Eggs and Ham* and *Sam I Am*. Later we progressed to the newspapers, but that was another story.

Lemmings

When she opened her eyes, nothing had changed. Ahead, the mirage still danced, an illusion of life in a dead landscape. The empty road stretched to infinity through the sun-bleached grass of the Nullarbor Plain.

'There's nothing beyond Ceduna,' was what her sister had said, and now Cynthia agreed with her. Why had Tom decided to buy a caravan and embark on this endless journey?

Before he had taken the package from work, he had always spoken disparagingly of retired people caravanning around Australia – he called it 'The Lemmings' Rush', and likened the grey nomads to the fabled lemmings of northern Europe, hell-bent on a journey to nowhere.

Cynthia had hoped – expected, even – that in retirement they would finally take their long-planned European trip but instead Tom had spent his money on a new car and a new caravan and then he had railroaded her into resigning from the job she loved. She still missed the office, the other girls, the morning teas and chats, the clients, even her boss. She would never forgive Tom. She tried to persuade herself that this was some sort of male menopause thing and eventually he would see reason and they could go home. She knew it was not so. When Tom made up his mind to do something, he would chase his goal forever. He had been like that when he was working, and he was like that now he was retired.

Mr Purviss had told her that there would always be a job for her if she wanted to come back to work. Cynthia sat in the passenger seat of the big four-wheel drive car, a car she lacked the skill to drive, wondering if she had the courage to get out at the next town, and catch a bus, or a train, or even a plane and fly back to Adelaide and sanity. Tom would never forgive her, of course, but did she really care? Her life was over and all she wanted was to escape from this existence.

Her head was throbbing again and she felt so stiff. She had been sitting in this car forever, she felt.

A wave of nausea struck her as they passed another dead kangaroo and the stench of corruption filled the vehicle. He would never get the stink out of his car, she thought with satisfaction. He said they couldn't run the air conditioning as it put too much strain on the engine while towing his caravan. The heat was unbearable. Damn Tom and his overbearing nature.

The sweat prickled on Cynthia's back and she was dreadfully afraid that she smelled. Tom certainly stank. And she did not know where they were, or what time it was because of the time difference between the two states. Were they in South Australia or in Western Australia or in some other benighted place? She could no longer be bothered looking at the map. This, she thought, is what hell must be like. If there was a hell, if there was a God. If Tom was ever going to go to heaven, she didn't want to go there with him. Till death do us part, she recalled. That's long enough. This wasn't a marriage, it was a life sentence.

'Where did we stay last night?' she asked him. 'I can't remember the town.'

'I can't remember either. These road stops on the Nullarbor are all the same. Look at your map.'

Reluctantly she picked up the crumpled paper. It was covered with blotches of something dark, perhaps coffee, all over it. Amazingly, Tom had relaxed his rule about not eating or drinking in his new car after the first few hundred kilometres.

'I *am* looking at the map and I can't work it out. We seem to have been on this road an eternity. How much further is Esperance?'

'First we get to Norseman and then we go to Esperance. Good fishing at Esperance.'

At Esperance, she knew, Tom would sit glassy-eyed on the jetty obsessed with catching a few little fish, while she cleaned his precious caravan. He was obsessive about the van. Was it at Port Lincoln or Streaky Bay where seagulls had landed on the roof and he had been furious lest they scratch it? He washed the outside at every opportunity and expected her to polish all interior surfaces and keep it like a palace.

Some holiday! A tin of Mr Sheen and rag, that was her lot in life. She had become a cleaner. She wished she was back at Pascoe and Pascoe typing legal documents as she had done for the past twenty-five years. She despaired of Esperance.

'It's always the same distance away,' said Tom.

'What is ?' she asked.

'The bloody mirage. As soon as you think you're getting near it, it disappears and then it comes back the same distance away as it was when you first saw it. They say you see some funny things out here at times. Remember the Nullarbor Nymph? There was supposed to be a naked woman running around. Truckies kept seeing her. They never did find her, though. That was ages ago, of course. Turned out to be a hoax in the end. It's amazing the crap some people believe.'

'Probably something like the *Flying Dutchman*,' Cynthia said. 'Wagner wrote an opera about it. A Dutch ship kept appearing off the Cape of Good Hope but no one could get close to it. The captain had cursed God or denied God so he was damned to sail around the Cape forever. Doomed to travel the same path, over and over, for eternity.'

She tossed the map aside and reached for the paper cup of coffee they had bought at the last road house. The coffee was cold, its surface congealed. She sighed, put the cup back in the round space the car designer had provided for it and continued talking. There was nothing else to do on this damned journey.

'People still see mirages of boats there and I think it's due to something called the inversion effect. You see a mirage of something that's somewhere else and the atmosphere reflects it into the area where you think you're seeing it.'

'Sounds like some sort of medieval European crap. Believe in God and you believe in devils. Doesn't work out here – bring those ideas into bright sunlight and you can discard them all. Denying a god that doesn't exist can't do you any harm, can it?'

'I don't believe in anything any longer,' said Cynthia, trying to restrain her tears. 'I'm even past faith, hope and charity. There's nothing but nothing out here. My sister was right about the Nullarbor.'

'I never did like Wagner anyway. Nasty, noisy cacophony.'

'Bits of his music are nice,' Cynthia began, but then she thought of the Wedding March from *Lohengrin*. That had been played at their marriage ceremony. Now she wished she had never heard it.

'What the hell is that?' demanded Tom.

The road ahead was blocked by a huge apparition. Distorted by the heat, it rose into the bright sky, occasionally disappearing into a cloud of white dust as the driver veered off on to the soft edges of the road. Watching it, Cynthia felt an odd sense of déjà vu. Surely they'd seen that thing before – even passed it before? Were there a lot of trucks like that on this road?

'Looks like a bloody big bell,' said Tom. 'I reckon it's mining equipment bound for Kalgoorlie – could be a huge crucible. Got a Wide Load sign on it. We'll just have to sit behind it. Can't risk passing it.'

'"It is a bell,"' quoted Cynthia, '"that summons thee to heaven or to hell."'

'What the hell are you on about?' asked Tom.

'It's a quote from *Macbeth*, but you wouldn't be interested. You're a Philistine anyway. That road train behind wants to pass us,' said Cynthia. 'He's coming up very fast – he'll overtake us and then the bell thing.'

'Shit!' screamed Tom. 'Bloody fool – get the video and take some footage of this. Hurry up – I want it for evidence. You're the legal secretary, aren't you?'

'Not any more,' snapped Cynthia. 'The camera's on the back seat. I'll have to take my seat belt off.'

It was when she was reaching for the video camera that the road train hit them. She heard the thunderous sound of impact, the sighing moan of the road train's brakes, and then the splintering, crumpling crash of the caravan's disintegration.

She felt elated while she was flying towards the windscreen, knowing that Tom's dream had shattered with the caravan. She would never polish it again. Perhaps now she could go home, even go back to work, have a normal life again. Then she knew absolute terror as she saw they were being propelled towards the truck bearing the crucible and realised that they would be crushed in the impact.

'Damn you to hell, Tom Holland!' she screamed.

Then there was merciful oblivion.

When she opened her eyes, nothing had changed. The headache was still there, aggravated no doubt, by the mirage that danced before the car. Ahead, the flat Nullarbor road stretched to infinity. She felt they had been travelling this road forever. Her body felt very stiff and the reek of corruption was worse than ever.

'I never did like Wagner,' Tom was saying.

'*The Flying Dutchman* was condemned to travel the same road again and again forever and forever,' said Cynthia. 'Do you suppose he thought he was dead and that he was haunting the place, or did he think he was still alive and just travelling on and on without hope of ever going home? Isn't it funny how when we wave at other cars, the passengers don't wave back?'

'It's just bad manners,' said Tom. 'It's an unwritten rule of the road that people wave at each other in the outback.'

'Why are they ignoring us?' persisted Cynthia. 'It's almost as if we're invisible.'

There was a huge truck blocking the road ahead. It seemed to rise into the dusty sky, its shape distorted by the heat that rose from the tarmac.

'That looks like a bloody big vehicle,' said Tom. 'It's probably got mining equipment for Kalgoorlie. We can't risk passing it. Only if we don't pass it, we'll be on this road forever.'

The Foundation Stone

'Thanks for that, mate.' Giovanni looked at the man who had volunteered himself as pallbearer. 'This bloke looks worse than Pete did when he was dying,' he thought.

The man's complexion was halfway between the grey of a heavy smoker and the liverish yellow of a chronic drinker. As the undertaker's men pushed the coffin into the vehicle, the stranger, breathing heavily, leaned against the hearse. Giovanni lingered, worried that the chap might collapse, but also because he was curious about the man's identity. Peter didn't have many friends.

Despite the warm spring sun, Giovanni shuddered. The idea of death made him uncomfortable. How long, he wondered, would it be before he too would be in a box, going straight to heaven or perhaps somewhere else. But not today, he thought.

He wiped his hands on his trousers to get rid of the feel of the coffin handle, and then reached out to shake the hand offered by the stranger. 'I didn't think we were going to have enough pallbearers for poor old Peter until you came forward,' he said.

'It's the least I could do,' replied the stranger. 'I'd lost touch with Pete over the years. I'd intended to try and catch up with him when I came to Adelaide. I had one hell of a shock when I saw his death notice in the newspaper. I'm over here visiting my daughter. I knew Peter back when he lived in Sydney.'

'That's years ago,' said Giovanni. 'Must be well over thirty years since Peter got back from New South Wales. Do you know Peter's sister, Prudence? She's my wife That's her, over there by the church door, sitting on the old foundation stone. She's not feeling too good. It's all been a bit of a shock. Peter was her younger brother. We knew he was crook, he had a bad heart, but we didn't expect him to go just yet. Makes you realise how short life is when something like this happens.'

'She's the lady who gave the eulogy, isn't she? She talked about how long the family has lived in this area and been involved with this parish. So he never married, did he? As I said, I only knew Peter in New South Wales. I can't say I ever met any of Peter's family,' said the man. 'I'm Bill Travers, by the way.'

'Pleased to meet you, Bill. Well, of course, not really pleased because of the circumstances. But any friend of Pete's is a friend of ours. I'm John Rossi. It's Giovanni, actually, but everyone calls me John. Come over and meet Prue.'

'So you're from Campbelltown, too, John? I suppose your roots go back as far as those trees up behind the church? I was looking at them before I came inside. Bloody big trees, those. They must have been here for a while.'

'The trees have been there for years, but I'm a Giovanni-come-lately, relatively speaking. My lot came over in 1956, four years before Campbelltown became a city. Prue's family arrived on the *Buffalo* back in 1800.'

'It wasn't the *Buffalo*, John, it was the *Buckinghamshire* in 1839,' said Prue wearily, rising from her seat on the rectangular stone that stood beside the door of the little chapel. 'I've told you that before. About twenty or thirty years before this church was built. St Martin's was one of the first churches built in Campbelltown. I'm Prudence, Peter's sister and John's wife. I heard you say your name is Bill Travers. I don't think we've met. How did you know Peter?'

'I'm sorry that you've lost your brother, Prue.' Bill extended his hand. 'Peter was a good mate of mine back in the old days. We shared a flat together for a while in Sydney. Both of us were going to write the great Australian novel, but neither of us did. Patrick White beat us to it. And we were a bit distracted from our writing by living, you might say. We could do anything back then, achieve anything. Or so Peter and I thought. I reckon they were the best years of our lives.'

'Not for my parents, they weren't,' snapped Prue. 'Those years that Pete was away from home were the worst years of their lives. None of us heard from him for months on end. We were all sure that he was in some sort of trouble. We didn't know if he was dead or alive or where he was, what he was doing or who he was with.'

'Yeah, a lot of the time Pete and I didn't know any of those things either,' said Bill ruefully.

'"The best of times and the worst of times",' said Giovanni wistfully.

'What are you talking about?' asked Prue.

'It's a quote from some book. By Dickens, I think,' said her husband. 'I'd have thought you would've recognised it. You're always telling me I should read more classics and less crime novels.'

'*A Tale of Two Cities*,' said Bill. 'You could say Pete's life was a tale of two cities, Adelaide and Sydney. Or Campbelltown and Sydney, if you want to be more specific. So you and Pete grew up here, did you Prue? Went to this church as kiddies, before it got turned into a funeral chapel?'

'Yes, this was St Martin's church when I was a child,' said Prue, watching sadly as the back door of the hearse was closed by the undertaker's assistant.

Giovanni patted her arm. The driver hesitated by the car door, looking in the family's direction.

'I reckon it's time we went into the church hall and had a cup of tea, love,' said Giovanni. 'Those blokes want to take Peter away now, but they're not supposed to drive off until we're out of the way.'

Prue collapsed against her husband's chest. 'I don't want to see him go,' she admitted. 'I still can't believe he's dead.'

Giovanni and Bill took an arm each and led Prue across the car park and down the steps out of the sunlight into the darkness of the hall.

'Looks like this hall was built in the 1970s,' said Bill, trying to make conversation. 'Is that when that big new church was built too? The cream brick job out in front with the St Martin's sign on it? I reckon I like that little old church better, though. It looks as if it's got real history. Convict-built, is it?'

'We didn't have convicts in South Australia,' said Prue, pulling her arm away from Bill's grip and glaring at him. 'That church was built by my ancestors and they were all free men and women. My people were farmers and orchardists. We had sheep and cattle and orange groves and later we had market gardens when the Italians came, and we built this country up from nothing.'

'And when us Italians came in, we taught you to eat pasta and pizza,' said Giovanni 'You sit down here. Keep an eye on her, Bill. I'll get you that cup of tea, love.'

Bill sat beside Prue. The silence was uncomfortable. He didn't want to raise the subject of Peter's bohemian past in Sydney lest he upset this woman further. The little chapel, or church as it was in Prue's childhood, seemed the safest ground.

'So St Martins was your parish church, was it?' he asked.

'Yes, my grandma used to talk about the harvest festivals they held here every autumn. The church was decorated with sheaves of wheat, bunches of grapes, apples, oranges, everything that grew in Campbelltown. It was a real farming community then, when my grandmother was a girl. Nothing like it is today, all built up with busy roads and shops. There were a lot less people then, so that little church was big enough. It only holds about fifty people, you know.'

'It's got lovely stained glass,' said Bill. 'Here's your husband with that cup of tea. Thanks, John, I didn't expect you to bring me one as well. No, I don't take sugar, black's fine. I'm supposed to watch my cholesterol, or so my daughter says. She's a bit bossy. She lives up near Morialta. The waterfall's pretty.'

'Are you staying with her for long?' Giovanni asked. 'You could come and have a meal with us. We've got the Italian restaurant just down the road, next to the gelateria. Prue makes a pretty good lasagne, for a sixth- or seventh-generation Aussie. I don't know how much cholesterol there is in it, though. But you can break the rules once in a while.'

'I don't really believe in trying too hard to follow the rules,' replied Bill. 'Never have. Neither did Peter.'

'Peter never followed any rules at all,' said Prue bitterly. 'He was the original hippie. I don't know what our ancestors would have thought of him. I don't suppose my brother ever told you that when our people first came to South Australia they were gardeners on Charles Campbell's property? He was the Scotsman that Campbelltown was named after. Those old pioneers, they understood hard work. They didn't spend their time sitting around smoking cigarettes and drinking tea and playing the guitar. I loved my brother, but he was a selfish man.'

'Pete wasn't one to smoke cigarettes much,' replied Bill, winking at Giovanni. 'Didn't spend much time drinking tea, either. True, he did play his guitar when he wasn't working on his novel. *Epoch of Belief*, that was what it was called. Did Pete ever talk about his book? Bloody good read, that story was. He did talk about his ancestors in it. There was a lot of stuff about religion and philosophy, and, now I come to think about it, a pretty good description of that little graveyard up behind the chapel. Of course, my own novel, *Season of Darkness*, that was brilliant, too. Mine was set in Sydney, so you could say we wrote tales of two cities. But Prue, there's no way I'd call Peter selfish. We shared everything, Pete and me.'

'I hate to tear you away from old friends, Prue dear, but Auntie Nance wants a word with you about Peter. She wants to know if you would like to have copies of some photographs she has.'

Prue rose and followed the elderly lady who had approached her.

'So what happened to those novels?' Giovanni asked. 'Were they ever published?'

'No, my wife burned both manuscripts in the fireplace in the flat. We were broke that winter and it was bloody cold. She said it was to keep the baby warm. Then she walked out on Pete and me and took the kiddy over to Adelaide to live with her parents. I've only just got in contact with young Hope again. That's why I'm here, picking up the pieces.'

'When you said you shared everything, you meant you shared expenses, I suppose.'

'More than that, mate. We shared our ink and paper, we shared our ideas, we shared booze, we shared our weed, and sometimes we shared our women. Don't tell Prue, but to be honest, I've never been certain whether Hope is my daughter or Peter's. Her mum's dead now, so it doesn't matter anyway. She looks mainly like her mum, but sometimes when I look at her I see Peter and sometimes I see me. Life's a strange thing, isn't it?'

Bill's mobile rang. 'Yes, love, I'm about finished here. I'll meet you out the front of the chapel. Hope doesn't trust me to drive in Adelaide,' he told Giovanni. 'She dropped me off and she's coming to pick me up, so I'll say goodbye. Thanks for your company. It's been much appreciated. Say goodbye to Prue for me. No hard feelings, but I reckon she'd rather not see me again.'

'So the foundation stone was left over from building the church,' Bill said to himself as he read the sign beside the rock. 'And the pioneers used it as a mounting block to climb up onto their horses. That would have been a sight to see. All those hardworking people, certain that they lived in the age of wisdom, dressed in their Sunday best, dark suits and white shirts and ladies in long dresses, big hats and gloves, resting from labour, gathered together to worship and gossip. Peter's ancestors congregated here in life, and then they were buried together in death. Nice continuity, that. If Pete was Hope's father, it's right that she lives here now. She came home, too. And Peter called his book *The Epoch of Belief*. It all makes sense now.'

He sat down on the stone where Prue had sat after the coffin had been carried out of the church. He looked towards the empty spot where the hearse had stood.

'Pete, I reckon your spirit never really left this place,' he said aloud. 'Even when you were in Sydney part of you stayed behind. And I've got to admit, I wouldn't mind my spirit haunting it too. It won't be long now before I'll be looking for a bit of permanence. I couldn't do better than stay here with young Hope and her kids, put down some roots like the big trees up the back there. It's not too late for that. I'll be a good grandpa to our kids, take them to the library, take them for walks in the park. And I'll take them hunting for tadpoles and yabbies in the creek like you said you used to do when you were a kiddie. And when the time comes, maybe I'll have my funeral here, too. It'll be something else we can share.'

Bill patted the stone. A foundation stone. A foundation was the beginning of things, not the end. The stone felt warm to his touch. Maybe it wasn't time to die yet. Hope would be here soon with her kids in the back of the car.

'You know what, Pete,' he addressed the wind in the trees, 'I'll get some good Scotch whisky, like the stuff we used to drink back in Sydney when we could afford it. That brand that we used to drink when we'd both had a good day writing, back when we still believed we'd both get the Nobel Prize for Literature. I'll bring it back here, and I'll bring two glasses. One for you, and one for me. We'll drink it together, mate. I'll pour your share on the ground, a libation to our stories, our souls and our memories. Maybe it's foolishness, but there's wisdom there, too. We'll drink to the best of times and the worst of times, just like your brother-in-law said.'

Ashes to Ashes

Jim was washing his car when I drove past. He waved me to stop.

'Where're you off to?' he demanded.

'I told you: Otto's funeral's this morning,' I said. 'Aren't you coming? You've lived next door to him for thirty years.'

'I called him the Nazi,' Jim sneered. 'My dad fought against them in the war.'

'The war's been over more than seventy years,' I said. 'The SS shot Otto's dad for criticising the Nazis. He told me about it.'

'Makes no difference,' said Jim, wiping his windshield. 'He had a German shepherd dog, too. Barked all the time.'

'So does your kelpie,' I said.

'The Nazis had those concentration camps,' said Jim, wringing his chamois. 'Gas chambers and incinerators.'

I shuddered.

Jim wiped his side mirrors. 'Going to be cremated, is he?'

At the funeral, I listened as Otto's younger brother, Johann, spoke of life in post-war Berlin. Starvation, malnutrition and death were rife. He, Otto and their mother lived in a damp cellar. Their mother, who had tuberculosis, died from the disease or perhaps from starvation. She insisted her boys needed food more than she did. The father, as I knew, was already dead, and Otto, at ten years old, was the man of the house. The two boys could not report their mother's death for fear of being placed in an orphanage and separated. And they knew dead paupers were tossed into muddy graves without coffins. Mutti deserved a coffin.

Otto, already streetwise, had supported the family by selling cigarettes on the black market. Now he redoubled his sales efforts in order to raise enough money to buy a coffin for Mutti. Seven-year-old Johann was given the task of keeping rats from attacking the corpse while Otto stood on wintery street corners selling cigarettes, always with one eye alert for the police.

Until they had sufficient to buy the coffin, the mother's body lay on her bed covered with a thin grey blanket. The coins that Otto brought home each night were placed at her feet. The boys hoped that if thieves came to the cellar they might think the woman was sleeping and not disturb her or the small horde of money. Fortunately it was a very cold winter, so Mutti did not smell too badly and no one came to investigate.

Fully clothed, the two boys shivered together at night beneath the only other blanket that they owned. The younger brother begged that they use the rug that covered their mother, but Otto insisted it would be disrespectful to take it from her. As the weeks passed, the children stopped lifting the cover to look at her face.

Eventually there was enough money to buy a pine box. Otto begged the loan of a handcart and together the children manhandled their mother into the coffin. How they got it up the stairs and onto the cart, Johann didn't explain.

Johann paused in his eulogy. 'There was not even one flower for our Mutti,' he said, glancing at the lilies and irises that covered Otto's coffin.

I drove home haunted by two skinny kids dragging a coffin through the snow to Berlin's over-crowded cemetery.

Jim was dead-heading his roses as I drove past. He raised his hand in greeting. I didn't stop to chat.

Ruh Fee Baladak

'It's all in the timing,' I told the kids who squatted with me beside the canal waiting for the ship. I used the patois that we all used, a polyglot language composed of Arabic, Italian, French and a little English. Before the war, everyone had a smattering of German, but now in Port Said in 1956, most of the Germans were gone and few people spoke that language.

'There was once a boy called Ahmed who mistook his timing,' said Mohammed. 'He was drawn into the propellers of a ship and the water turned red from his blood. His body was never found.'

'Did his family not complain to the authorities?' asked Johnny, the English boy. 'Was there not a riot in the streets?'

Johnny's father had been replaced as adviser to the Egyptian police force. Tomorrow Johnny and his family would leave for England.

'No, Ahmed was a boy of the bazaar,' said Mohammed, shrugging. 'His father was dead and he had no uncles. Um Ahmed, his mother, grieved, but there was no family of note to lament his loss. Of course, if I, or even Tony here, were killed, there would be much trouble.' He nudged my bare ribs and grinned at me, then turned back to Johnny. 'But Tony and I know what we are doing. We never mistake our timing.'

Darkness oozed along the sand towards us. The vessel was coming closer. My heart thumped in rhythm with the sound of the huge engines. The smell of oil filled my nostrils. I swallowed, hoping my audience would not sense my fear. I watched carefully as the level of the darkening water ahead of the prow fell, sucked under the ship by the screws. The high superstructure of the boat hid the sun. I shivered.

'Are you afraid?' shouted Maurice, over the noise of the ship's engines.

Next week, I knew, he and his family would be in Marseilles.

'You have goose-pimples.'

'No, I am cold,' I said. 'I shiver when the ship blocks out the light. But it will soon pass and there will be warmth again.'

'You are not as cold as Johnny will be when he goes to London,' Mohammed told me. 'Or even Maurice in France, although it is said the south of France is warmer than Paris. Italy, of course, can be quite hot, although snow, I have read, occurs in the north. I am the only one who will still be here for the summer. I shall think of you all and pity you who live in the grey cold of Europe.'

I wondered why Mohammed wanted to swim the canal. I was doing it because the other boys had heard me boast that I had swum between the ships. They had dared me to do it again in their presence. At fifteen, I could not refuse a dare.

But there was no reason for Mohammed to take this risk. He cared nothing for those other lads. I was his only true friend. Suddenly I realised that Mohammed was endangering his life because of me, because of our friendship.

'I am not going to Europe,' I told him. 'My father has decided that we will go to Australia. It is said that Australia is a hot country like Egypt.'

The warmth and light of the sun returned as the ship passed. Carefully, Mohammed and I watched the ship's wake. This was the critical moment. Too soon, we would be dragged into the propellers and die as Ahmed had died. Too late, and there would be no time to cross the canal before the next vessel bore down on us.

This was the narrowest part of the Suez Canal, just before it widened and opened out to form the Bitter Lakes where convoys of ships anchored to await permission to proceed into that part of the canal that led to Suez, Aden and the open sea. But even here it's a long way to the other side, I thought, gazing at the stretch of blue water between the white sand where we sat and where the buoy on the opposite bank bobbed. And it must be done quickly before the next ship arrives.

But I knew it was possible. I remembered also that the last time that I had swum between the ships I had sworn never to do it again. I recalled how my lungs had burned and I remembered the cramping pain in my arms and legs, and how I had prayed to Saint Antony, my patron saint, and promised the saint that if I survived the ordeal I would never again do anything so foolish. Now, for bravado, I was about to break my vow and risk my life. And risk not only my life, but Mohammed's life too.

'*Salvami, Sant'Antonio*,' I prayed. 'Even if I don't deserve your help.'

Now was the moment.

'*Yallah!*' yelled Mohammed, '*Yallah!*'

Together we dived, cutting in unison through the blue water, stroke for stroke, breath for breath. His brown body and my paler one were in perfect synchrony; we might have been two pistons in a machine, so perfectly matched were we. Behind us, I knew that the boys were cheering, but I hardly heard their voices. I had no need to watch Mohammed; I knew that he would not leave my side, nor I his, until we reached the far side of the canal.

It was just as the last time had been. My chest hurt; my lungs were bursting. I could not maintain the pace. I could swim no further. But with Mohammed churning beside me, surrender was impossible. If I sank beneath the waters, so would he.

Breathe, stroke, breathe, stroke, breathe, stroke.

'*Sant' Antonio, dove sei?*' I begged, I prayed. Surely the end must be near. Surely it must soon be over. Was it this far, the last time I had done it?

Something loomed in the water ahead. Something straight and metallic with a round base that rose and fell with the waves. I reached out a hand and grasped the rail. We had reached the buoy on the eastern side of the Suez Canal.

Mohammed's head surfaced beside mine. 'I feared that I would die,' he grinned.

'I also,' I said.

'Allah was gracious,' he said.

'As was also Saint Antony,' I replied. 'Together, we have crossed from Africa to Asia. My father says the canal marks the border of two continents.'

'And soon you will travel to another far continent,' said Mohammed. 'I have heard there is gold in Australia. When you become a rich man, will you send for me?'

'Of course, my brother,' I promised. 'We will share a villa overlooking the sea with a tennis court for my Maraya. There will be feasts and dancing girls. But,' I remembered, 'my father says there are no dancing girls in Australia. There are, of course, kangaroos.'

In truth, I knew little about Australia and dreaded our departure. My Lebanese mother wished to return to her homeland where her family owned orchards and farms, but my Italian father wanted to go to Italy. At the end of one dreadful fight, my father had snatched our passports and stormed out of our apartment, returning with the news that he had arranged with the Australian consul for our immigration to Australia.

If it was a victory for him, it was a Pyrrhic one; I do not think my mother ever forgave him his impulse. Mama settled into a sulky silence punctuated by attacks of hysteria as my father disposed of any possessions he deemed unnecessary or unsuitable for life in the Antipodes. The news that there would be no servants in Australia drove her to further torrents of desperate tears; although before our friends and neighbours, unwilling to admit her defeat, my mother spoke with enthusiasm of our departure for our new country.

After another ship had passed and the water had regained its equilibrium, Mohammed invoked Allah's help and I made the sign of the cross. We struck out again for Africa.

The air on the bus back to Port Said was thick with Woodbine cigarettes, the smell of packed humanity and the fusty smell from caged chickens that some of the veiled women carried on their knees.

A man in a *gallabiah* leaned close to me and yelled, '*Ruh fee baladak!*'

I shrugged. 'This is my country,' I replied. 'I was born here, as was my father.'

'Your father is Italian,' whispered Mohammed.

'He is registered with the Italian consulate, but he was born in Egypt,' I said. 'My grandfather came here just after the French and the English built the canal.'

'This boy is my friend,' Mohammed told the man. 'I do not wish to hear anyone tell him "Go back to your country." Do not say *ruh fee baladak* to him.'

'He is an intruder. We do not want Europeans in Egypt. They have stolen our jobs. The English take the money that the ships pay to transit the canal. Egypt is exploited by foreigners. *Yallah, effendi, ruh fee baladak!*'

He rummaged in his clothing and I saw the glint of steel. Mohammed grasped my arm and tugged me toward the bus door.

Angry and foolhardy, I turned and opened my mouth to reply but Mohammed urged me to get off the bus with him.

'He may follow us,' said Mohammed, looking back. 'We must flee. Such fanatics are dangerous.'

We ran through the narrow alleys of the bazaar, dodging donkey carts, bicycles, faceless women bearing burdens on their heads, and men carrying trays piled with Arab bread. I smelled the fragrance of cumin and coriander. I wondered if there would be *molohiah* and *falafel* in Australia.

'I would give you something, Tony,' said Mohammed. He thrust half a coin at me. 'I have divided this silver coin with the head of King Farouk. See, I have drilled a hole in it and attached a cord so you can wear it around your neck. I will keep half and you will keep half. When we meet again, the halves will be reunited.'

'Farouk is no longer in favour. You should have used a coin with the face of Colonel Nasser,' I joked.

Mohammed looked sad.

I hugged him. 'I will treasure it until we meet again.'

'*In sha'Allah*,' he said.

We heard loud music over the hubbub of the streets; the high tinny sound of the Arab flute, drums, the nasal inflection of song. Our passage was blocked by a large marquee hung with gaudy flags. I paused to see why a crowd had gathered.

'A rich man has visited Mecca and a cow will be sacrificed. Let us go, Tony. This is not for your eyes,' urged Mohammed.

'But I am Egyptian,' I said.

He shook his head. 'This is the action of the peasants, Tony. You have mixed only with people of the better class, people like me and my family. Come away, my brother.'

But I lingered. Soon I would leave Egypt and the hidden knowledge of the streets would be lost to me. I wished to know and to feel all that the land of my birth could show me.

A cow was led into the space before the marquee. She turned to look at me with puzzled eyes. Two men tugged at cords attached to her front legs. Bellowing a protest, she fell to her knees. I saw the whites of her eyes. Her nostrils flared in fear. She groaned as men pushed her head to face Mecca. Swiftly the mullah did his work. I gasped at the wound in the beast's slashed throat. A scarlet stream flowed towards me, coagulating as it flowed over the hot cobblestones. I smelled blood and faeces.

'I must go. My family awaits me,' I yelled at Mohammed and fled, fighting nausea.

At our apartment, Uncle Karam and my parents sat on the balcony drinking Greek coffee and eating *baalawa*. The last rays of the sun glowed red on our best cups and silverware and on the bald head of our honoured guest. He was not really my uncle but was our landlord, a good friend of our family, and the father of Maraya, whom I had loved since I reached the age of five.

'*Vraiment, cette une crise grande,*' Uncle Karam was saying. He preferred French and always declined to speak the local patois. His Italian was better than Papa's. He spoke the purest Arabic I ever heard. When he learned that we would live in Australia, he taught me English with an Oxford accent.

He was a Copt. The Copts were renowned for their education and their wealth. Papa had told me that they were descended from the Pharaohs; that they lived in Egypt long before the Arabs invaded the Peninsula in the sixth century. The Copts, my father said, were an ancient Christian sect. I often thought that Uncle Karam's bald head looked like the mummy of the Pharaoh Rameses. And that Maraya, who had ever been beautiful beyond her years, resembled Nefertiti.

'Is Maraya here?' I asked, looking about the apartment eagerly.

'She is playing tennis,' said Uncle Karam.

He looked at Papa. 'Nasser needs money to build the Aswan dam so he will nationalise the canal.'

'There will be war,' said Papa gloomily. 'The prime minister of Britain threatens it. The Arabs will cut the throats of any Europeans who remain. My Jewish friends have already fled.'

'You have come from the bazaar, Antoine?' Uncle Karam asked me. 'What is the mood of the people?'

'They told me *ruh fee baladak,*' I said. I did not mention the cow.

'I wish I had a country to go back to,' Uncle Karam said sadly. 'We Copts are not popular with the Arabs.'

'You should go to France, my friend,' said my father. He sighed. 'If only you could come to Australia with us.'

Uncle Karam shrugged. 'France, or perhaps Algeria, but not Australia. We are the wrong colour. Australia has the White Australia policy. But Egypt is my land. I am tied to it by history, by blood and by possessions. I must stay here and trust in God.'

'I trust only distance,' said my father grimly.

'But you must come with us. What if Maraya forgets me?' I pleaded. 'Surely this matter of colour is not important in Australia? What of the Aborigines? Are they not black?'

'It is Australian law,' said my father sadly. 'Only those with white skin are allowed entry. Preference is given to the British, but Europeans are permitted. As for the Aborigines, I have heard they are badly treated.'

I gasped. What sort of land was this in which we would live?

'Maraya will never forget you,' Uncle Karam said. 'Could Héloïse forget Abelard, or Juliet forget Romeo? When there is peace, when you are a man, you will return for her. You and my daughter will live together in Europe or perhaps Australia will relax her laws regarding colour. But Egypt is too dangerous for you, my son. The Arabs are volatile.'

'It will be a beautiful wedding,' said Mama, smiling as she poured Uncle Karam another cup of thick, dark coffee from the copper bric.

There was not a lot of furniture left in our home on the evening a week later when we heard a frantic hammering at the door of our apartment. We were sitting around the new table with folding legs that Papa had commissioned a carpenter make. Most of our belongings had been sold to pay for the voyage but Papa was determined that both here and in Australia his family would sit at a table to eat as Christians should.

Papa had served the pasta into our bowls and Mama was pouring thick red tomato sauce over it. This made me queasy, because I was reminded of the cow's blood. The sacrifice still haunted my dreams.

Again, the pounding on our door.

'The Arabs have come to murder us!' cried Mama, dropping the ladle.

The metal spoon hit the table. Red splatter covered Papa's white shirt.

'Protect your mother!' shouted Papa. He grabbed the bread knife and ran to the door.

I picked up the ladle and pushed Mama behind me, although I knew that my skinny frame would hide little of her ample body.

My father listened at the door. Recognising the voice of our Greek neighbour, Papa opened the door just a crack and Mr Petridis, one arm around his weeping wife and the other holding his screaming baby, pushed forward and the family fell into our apartment. Papa glanced out into the hallway, then slammed the door and bolted it.

'Signor Rossi!' Mr Petridis shouted, 'Our landlord has been murdered. The Arabs attacked the Copts with machetes.'

'No,' wailed Mama. 'It cannot be possible.'

Mr Petridis continued, his voice shaking, 'The Copts had sought sanctuary in their church but there was no mercy. Karam Hennis and his family were among those who were slaughtered. No one is safe in Egypt, not even the Copts.'

Papa rushed to close the shutters and put out all the lights. We huddled together, the dark room lit by one small candle. My father brought out his last bottle of cognac and poured generous measures. Even I was permitted alcohol that night.

Mamma and Mrs Petridis wept, clutched each other and tried to muffle the baby's cries. Papa and Mr Petridis conferred, speaking softly in Greek. My Greek was never good, but I was sure I heard the word 'rape'. I moved my chair closer but my father pushed me away.

What horrors had happened to Maraya and her family? Was Uncle Karam's head split like the head of Farouk on the coin at my throat? Did blood flow like that of the slaughtered cow? And Maraya – my beautiful Maraya – what of her? My chest was tighter than when I had swum the canal. I was suffocating. I fell to the floor, my hands over my face.

'Papa, we must find Maraya and take her to Australia with us,' I sobbed when I could speak again.

'Maraya is dead, Antonio,' said Papa.

'No!' I shrieked.

Papa slapped my face and poured cognac down my throat.

'And then they set fire to it,' said Mr Petridis, his words seeming to come from a great distance.

The ship had traversed the Bitter Lakes, had passed Suez and Aden.

We were in the open sea now, bound for Australia. There would be no further landfall until we reached Fremantle, and we would not disembark even there, for Melbourne was our destination.

As the sun rose, Papa and I stood by the rail and watched dolphins dance ahead of us in the calm water.

Alone in our cabin, Mama either slept or wept. She had spoken little since we had left our home. When she did speak, it was to recite a litany of betrayal and loss.

'It is said that to see dolphins in the dawn brings good fortune and great joy,' said Papa in Arabic.

'I shall never speak Arabic again,' I said in sudden rage. 'Never again shall I hear those words *ruh fee baladak*. In Australia no one will speak thus. We go to our new home in a new land.'

I thrust my hand into my pocket and drew out the last of my Egyptian money. I showed the coins to my father. I hurled them as far I could. The rising sun turned the silver to gold. Would there indeed be gold in Australia as Mohammed had predicted? Tiny splashes showed where the missiles hit the water.

'And what of the coin around your neck that your friend Mohammed, he who you called brother, gave you?' asked Papa.

I touched the talisman. The dolphins disappeared behind my tears.

About the Stories

The term 'terra nullius' is a lie. Australia was not an 'empty land' when it was annexed by the British in 1788. But the perception of the continent as empty persisted in the colonists' minds – somehow they overlooked both the presence of the indigenous people and the patina of time over the engravings on rock faces that evidenced a long historical presence by the first inhabitants. It is to Australia's shame that it took until 1992 when the Mabo vs Queensland case established native land rights.

That said, you will notice that there are no stories in this collection from the point of view of indigenous people. Although I am sixth-generation Australian and call this land mine, I do not feel that I have the right or the qualification to assume the mindset of the first people of Australia. This is a collection of stories from the point of view of the invaders, some of whom are aware of and sympathetic to the indigenous people – for example, Hugh Foulkes in the title story and Tony and his father in the last story. But the majority of the characters in these stories seem quite unaware and unmindful of the presence of the Aborigines and of their plight, as are most Australians today.

Most of the stories in this collection deal with the theme of travelling, whether as stories told by people moving across the Australian landscape or as migrants coming to terms with a new country. All but two of them have won competitions and all but two have been published elsewhere. As my husband says, that is eight out of ten of the stories that have achieved some sort of recognition. I apologise if you, the reader, have encountered them before. I was prompted to publish them because recently my ancient computer crashed (although it was miraculously restored to life by my son David with minimal damage done). A few stories that could very well have been included (sorry, Laurie Anderson, your favourite – 'Sic Transit Gloria Mundi' – was among them) disappeared forever. I realised then how easily writing can be lost and decided to put this collection together.

Terra Nullius

This story is told from the point of view of my ancestor Hugh Foulkes, who was one of Captain Charles Sturt's bullock drivers on the expedition in search of the mythical Inland Sea in 1844. I have perhaps given Hugh the insight I would like him to have had – but that is my literary licence. For an excellent account of the Sturt expedition, I recommend *Sturt's Desert Drama* by Ivan Rudolph, published in 2006 by the Queensland University Press. 'Terra Nullius' was runner-up at the Clare Writers' Festival in 2014.

The Memory Lingers Still

This story was the first of my published stories. It won first prize in November 1998 in a creative writing competition (long before the Salisbury Writers' Festival began) organised by the City of Salisbury and was published in a small anthology called *The Spirit of Salisbury*. It is, no doubt, out of print, but I treasure my copy of the anthology. It tells of the distillation of alcohol but also of friendship and there is a grain of truth in that story, as there is in all the stories in *Terra Nullius*. My husband Frank, to whom this book is dedicated, appears in this tale under the pseudonym of Charles.

Nemesis

This story has never been entered in a competition, or indeed previously published. My daughter Francesca read it and told me, 'It's a winner, Mum,' and Brenda Matthews tells me it is her favourite story in the collection. It was inspired by my love of Greek culture and the idea that cultural assimilation can work both ways. And there is a lot of travel in it – Port Lincoln to Darwin to Alice Springs – as one of the characters seeks, like Oedipus, to evade fate by flight.

Holiday of a Lifetime

This is another of my early efforts. Many years ago, *The Advertiser* used to run a short story competition with a very short word count allowed. The stories were published in the paper during the summer months and cheery subjects were preferred. This story has a happy veneer but it does, like much of my work, have a dark undercurrent. Nevertheless, it won me a David Jones voucher, with which I bought a toaster which must be fifteen years old but which still works well.

Sangue di Terra

This story was entered in the Wirra Wirra Vineyards short story competition in 2005 and published in the anthology *Time Fractures*. It is a little boastful to state that the judges that year were J.M. Coetzee (Nobel Prize winner and twice Booker Prize winner), Katherine England, reviewer for *The Advertiser*) and Alan Smith, Director of the State Library of South Australia, but their names are listed in the anthology and there is nothing like a bit of reflected fame. My experiences in vineyard work coloured this story but the incident of the dead backpackers is fiction. Once again, my love of the mythology of ancient Greece features.

Reading Between the Lines

In 2012 Barbara Wiesner and Jude Aquilina, who were then with the SA Writers' Centre, suggested to me that I enter the National Year of Reading Short Story Competition. The theme was 'It's never too late to learn to read'. I wrote 'Reading Between the Lines', which used the persona of an elderly Chinese lady who lived next door to me and who made *bao* for my son David. I sent the entry off and forgot about it. I was a bit perturbed when I received an email from Tasmania that said, 'Congratulations, please send your bank details.' I nearly deleted the email in the belief that it might be sort some of Tasmanian Nigerian bank scam, but then I remembered that the competition I had entered was administered by the Tasmanian Writers' Centre. I phoned them and was told that I had won the South Australian division of the national competition. Thanks, Barbara and Jude!

Lemmings

In 2002, Australian Roadside Services ran a competition with the theme of 'road'. 'Lemmings' was published in the anthology *Slippery When Wet* in 2002 and republished the following year as part of a four-volume collection of short stories. The grain of truth in this story is that Frank and I did travel across the Nullarbor plain and were stuck behind a huge truck carrying what was probably a huge bucket destined for the mines of Kalgoorlie. The thought 'what if' inspired the rest of the tale.

The Foundation Stone

This won the Campbelltown Literary Award in 2011. The theme of the award demands that the story be set in the Campbelltown area, and I found inspiration in a small chapel which is situated behind St Martins, the current Anglican church. The smaller building predates the newer one by many years and was built by the pioneers of the district. The chapel was, at the time, rented by a funeral director. When I attended a funeral there, I saw a large square stone by the door of the church and was told that the early settlers had used it to mount their horses. This was the foundation of the story which tells of two writers who both aspired to write The Great Australian Novel.

Ashes to Ashes

This has never been entered in an award or been published. It is based on a story that I heard from a friend and which touched my heart. As always, fiction embellishes truth.

Ruh Fee Baladak

This was long-listed for the second David Harold Tribe Fiction Award at Sydney University in 2014. Brenda Matthews describes it as 'the dark story' and thought it might have been autobiographical because of its graphic nature. No, Brenda, the story is not autobiographical, but it is almost biographical, albeit with the overlay of fiction. It recounts incidents told to me by my husband Frank, who is given the persona of Tony and who did, indeed, swim between the ships in the Suez Canal and who, like Tony, had to hurriedly leave Egypt in 1956 at the time of the Suez Crisis. 'Ruh fee baladak' is Arabic for 'Go back to your country' – words that were often said to Tony (and Frank) before their departures. And words, indeed, the Aborigines in the first story might have said to Captain Sturt's party as they trampled roughshod through the waterholes of central Australia. I was tempted to give the collection this name, but thought it might be too obscure for non-Arabic speakers, and could be misconstrued by those who know the language.

I hope you enjoy these stories of travel, of migration, of the settlement of South Australia and of the diverse peoples and cultures of our home.

Margaret Visciglio, March 2015

Acknowledgements

My thanks to my long-suffering husband Frank, who puts up with the forgotten meals and the lack of company that always accompany my absences in far-flung places of the spirit. The body is present but the mind is absent! In small recompense, I dedicate this book to him with all my love.

Thanks as always to Stephen Matthews and the lovely Brenda of Ginninderra Press, who encouraged me in this enterprise to gather together stories I have written over the years. I wanted to present the idea that Australia has been settled by a diverse group of people but also to pay homage to the fact that we were not the first to come here and that we owe a debt to the past.

And very great thanks to my son David, who rescued my ageing computer and its contents from what could have been a Stygian oblivion. To have one's work suddenly disappear before one's eyes borders on Greek tragedy, but to see most of it resurrect is a miracle indeed. A warning to all writers – back your stuff up! There were at least three stories that might have been included in this anthology that I cannot locate anywhere.

Thank you to Symon Williamson and to the Tea Tree Gully Library, who generously offer their assistance and their hospitality for book launches – we Ginninderra writers appreciate you immensely and would be lost without your help and the use of the area Symon refers to as the Relaxed Reading Area but which I call the Ken Vincent Room.

Indeed, thank you to all the wonderful councils who run literary awards and competitions which encourage writers and writing. The Campbelltown Literary Award people, including Jill Whittaker, Deputy Mayor, have been extremely kind to me – I hesitate to enter their competition again since in 2014 I won not only my section but the overall prize! The Salisbury Writers' Festival has operated now for ten years and I commend them. Clare is a recent entry to the Festival scene and Meredith Appleyard, Nan Berrett and Nigelle-ann Blaser are marvellous people who run a terrific festival.

But most of all, thank you to my readers. Without you, there would be no point in writing. Since writing is my passion, you give meaning to my life. Thank you for that.

Margaret Visciglio

9 781740 279321